Murder in the Lab

Leonid Heifets

DORRANCE
PUBLISHING CO
EST. 1920
PITTSBURGH, PENNSYLVANIA 15222

Dorrance Publishing Co
701 Smithfield Street
Pittsburgh, PA 15222
Visit our website at *www.dorrancebookstore.com*

ISBN: 978-1-4809-0939-7
eISBN: 978-1-4809-0801-7

Contents

Other Books by Leonid Heifets

From Russia with Tales and Confessions to Discovering America,
2009, Dorrance Publishing

African Exposure,
2010, Tate Publishing

The Second Coming of the White Plague,
2012, Tate Publishing

Cast of Characters

Mr. Edward Clinton - Vice President of the Institute

Dr. Jim Dellinger - Executive Director
of the Department of Diagnostic Laboratories

Dr. Derrick Meyer - Director of Operations

Dr. Charles Higgins - Chairman, Department of Medicine

Dr. David Brinkley - Director of the Core Diagnostic Laboratory

Dr. Chuck Crowley - Director of the Microbiology/
Virology Diagnostic Laboratory

Dr. Michael Gilman - Director of the
Pharmacology Diagnostic Laboratory

Dr. Henry Frontier - Director of the TB Diagnostic Laboratory

Dr. Peter Vincent - Director of the
Immunology Diagnostic Laboratory

Dr. Bharat Gupta - Director of the
Molecular Diagnostic Laboratory

Dr. Maryann Sandoval - Director of the
Genetics Research Laboratory

Dr. Boris Filatov - Virologist, Researcher in the
Microbiology Laboratory

Mrs. Rebecca (Becky) Brown - Supervisor in the Microbiology Laboratory

Mrs. Gloria West - Administrative Assistant to Dr. Derrick Meyer

Mr. Rashid Siddiqi - Police Inspector

Mr. Andrew Powell - FBI Agent

Mr. Jim Galen - FBI Agent

Ms. Clare Whitcomb - FBI Agent

Mr. Mark Griffin - FBI Special Agent

Mr. Patrick McMahon - Technical Inspector of Autoclaves

Ms. Maria Gonzales - Friend of Mr. McMahon

Chapter 1 -

Found Dead in the Car

In a park outside the city of Greeneville, Montana, barbeque smoke mingled with the June haze. The air was redolent with caramelized onions, grilled tomatoes, hamburgers, and lemonade. In the parking lot next to the park, glistening under the hot bright sun, sat a black Lincoln Town Car with its motor running. The cold air inside the car continued to blow on the lifeless body slumped over the steering wheel. The deceased was Dr. Derrick Meyer, Director of Operations in the Department of Diagnostic Laboratories at the Research Institute for Applied Immunology.

This was just the beginning of a drama that would unfold over the next weeks and months, the likes of which the small community of Greeneville had never seen.

• • • • •

In a small clearing nearby, standing beside a lonely oak tree where a sizable crowd was talking and laughing, a young lab technician was becoming bored with the social scene, and a little annoyed by a variety of aromas permeating the air.

A little way off, an older man by the name Dr. David Blankley, Director of the Core Laboratory, was telling a young woman stories about his days as boy during the Great Depression and World War II. He had had fantasies of joining the army to fight the Germans, but he was much too young. His mother, wise woman that she was, kept him safely at home and in school. Alas, he grew up, and got his chance to serve in Korea, where he was captured as a prisoner of war. While there, he explained, he learned to speak Korean, and he now began singing some old Korean folk song. In the meantime, he wondered if there was any more non-alcoholic beer in the cooler, or if he'd taken the last of it.

The woman that he was talking to pretended to listen with great interest. She was trying with all her might not to give away her utter boredom. She hoped someone or something would rescue her from this man's attention. Finally, he started singing, and she tried not to look too embarrassed.

Dr. Chuck Crowley, an unmarried man, was sitting on a bench just fifteen feet behind Blankley, chuckling as he watched the young woman's reaction. She was, in fact, quite attractive, with long, blonde curls and bright blue eyes, pale skin, and a slim but curvy figure. He remembered her from a meeting sometime before; he tried to recall her name, but failed. Thinking that she works in the same department, he decided he would check in on the office sometime during the next week. Perhaps her name was Tatiana something?

The haze continued to sit heavily, as if threatening to actually fall and crush those lingering beneath it. A long-legged young woman dressed in white was quickly walking toward the black Town Car. She glanced inside the car and suddenly stepped back, horrified by what she saw.

She screamed, "Somebody, call the Security Office. It's Derrick! I can't open the door. Somebody help! He's…he's *dead!*"

The woman's cry for help was muffled by the haze and the noise of the crowd. She rushed back to the party and quickly got the attention of the crowd. The woman was the administrative assistant to Dr. Meyer at the Research Institute for Applied Immunology.

Twenty minutes later, the department's annual June picnic was a crime scene. Top administrators and a swarm of police officers converged around the car, and a person with an appearance and tone of authority took charge and gave directions. An ambulance and a large truck arrived at the scene. Cars near Derrick's car were towed away, and spectators were ordered to move behind the yellow crime scene tape. Two paramedics dressed in a full protective gear and respirators emerged from the ambulance, removed Derrick's body from the car, and zipped it inside a black body bag. The car was moved into the truck. The ambulance bearing Derrick's body and the truck proceeded to the regional CDC facility.

In addition to his employment at the Institute, Derrick had a job as a microbiologist at the Bozeman Deaconess Hospital where his wife, Sharon, also worked as a nurse. Sharon had a penchant for the finer things in life, so when she insisted on living in a luxury apartment, Derrick consented even though it meant working a second job. After his promotion to the Director of Operations with a substantial increase of his salary, Derrick had intended to quit this part-time job, but he put off making that decision.

The day before the picnic, as a function of this additional job, Derrick had participated in an autopsy on a man who recently came from India and died suddenly. It was thought that he might have died from a stroke, but that was not confirmed at the autopsy. His death was listed as 'cause of death unknown,' and a suspicion was brought up by the State Health Department epidemiologist that the person might have had a dangerous infection. People who were involved in dealing with this patient from India were placed in quarantine. As a microbiologist, Derrick's task was to inoculate in culture media the tissue samples taken at autopsy, and subsequently to identify the organism if any bacteria grew from these samples. It was suggested that Derrick's sudden death could have been caused by an unknown infection contracted from dealing with the tissue from the deceased man. As a precautionary measure and for appropriate examination, Derrick's body was transported to the regional CDC facility.

The Institute for Applied Immunology was established with the purpose of addressing new research directions leading to future medicine. These included development of new molecular diagnostic methods and gene therapy tools, as well as for new approaches to treat various immunological disorders. Favorable conditions for creating the Institute offered by the State of Montana, on one hand, and a possibility of recruiting top scientists to this new place, on the other, led to selection of a site next to the city of Bozeman. The top scientists recruited to the Institute also enriched the Medical Educational Program at the State University in Bozeman as affiliated faculty members, which led to an opportunity to become a full-scale medical school from the current partnership program with the University of Washington, School of Medicine.

The new campus consisted of a number of buildings, and more new ones were still under construction. Diagnostic laboratories were housed in two of these buildings. The city of Greeneville grew around the Institute's campus, and became connected, at the same time, to the city of Bozeman. Population growth stimulated an increase in the number of people employed, development of various small businesses, tourism, and even development of a symphony orchestra situated in a newly built concert hall, not very large but with remarkably good acoustics. The Institute attracted both semi-retired older generation scientists and younger people seeking the opportunity to get involved in research. It also opened a wide range of employment opportunities for graduates from Montana universities. All these activities were a part of efforts by a small group of enthusiastic businessmen and scientists to promote the future of this 'Big Sky Country' state.

Greeneville and Montana, in general, is a pretty quiet place. Anytime something unusual happens, like a man found dead in the front seat of his car, everyone and their grandmother jumped to the conclusion it must have been a homicide. A whole score of police officers had shown up at the small field southwest of the city to investigate Dr. Meyer's death. Not long after, a group of people from the regional FBI came and assumed command of the investigation.

The party was shut down and the remaining food and drinks were seized and taken to the regional CDC laboratories.

An emergency meeting was convened in the office of the Vice President for Administrative Affairs Mr. Edward Clinton, with participation of three FBI agents and top management of the Department of Diagnostic Laboratories, in which Derrick had been employed as Director of Operations.

One of the visitors, a man without any distinctive features — tall, muscular, and smoothly shaved, wearing a grey suit, said in a low voice, "My name is Andrew Powell; I'm with the regional office of the Federal Bureau of Investigation. These are Agent Clare Whitcomb and Agent Jim Galen. Needless to say, the sudden death of Dr. Meyer is quite a challenge for us. Aside from the possibility that it was due to unknown natural causes, we may also consider two other possibilities. One is an unknown infection contracted by Dr. Meyer when he was working with tissue specimens obtained from the body of a person who came from India and died from an unknown cause. This is the reason that the body was taken to the special CDC facility, and a few people who have been in close contact with Dr. Meyer during the past two days have been placed into quarantine."

Dr. Crowley suggested that Mr. Powell tell the group the background for having and using the CDC facility and all the unusual settings.

"Perhaps some of you are well-informed as to why we have regional CDC facilities around the country," stated Powell. "You may remember that on September 18 of 2001, one week after the September 11 attacks, letters containing anthrax spores were mailed around the country, infecting seventeen people and killing five others. Eventually, the perpetrator was identified as Bruce Ivins, a microbiologist who worked in Fort Detrick. He had some mental health problems and committed suicide in 2008, which ended the investigation. Many experts still doubt the validity of the conclusion that Ivins was the perpetrator. Although the episode was not connected to terrorism as originally suspected, it was a wake-up call, because there is a potential threat of a terrorist attack with biological or chemical weapons. As you know, thousands of people were involved in the development of such weapons in the past in the former Soviet Union, and many scientists in other countries, including those in the Middle East who used to support terrorists, have been trained in this field, and such weapons are still being developed there. So far, no terrorist attacks using biological weapons have taken place in the U.S., but some alerts and precautions are necessary.

"The autopsy and testing of Meyer's body were performed at the regional CDC facility in units with Bio-Safety Level 4 practices (BSL-4), which includes special architectural design of the laboratories, quite a sophisticated ventilation system, and rigorous protective measures are in place for the people working there."

"Is that the only reason why the FBI and CDC have taken over the investigation?" asked someone in the group.

"No, there is another reason, as well. Although no terrorist attack using chemical or biological weapons has taken place in the U.S., there have been attempts by some individuals with mental problems working in a few diagnostic and research laboratories to poison or infect their colleagues. I am not implying that it happened here, but the possibility of murder is always on the table in cases of sudden unexplainable death, especially in places where dangerous agents like poisonous chemicals or bacteria are available. Please keep this discussion confidential and ask your employees to be calm and not to spread any rumors. I would suggest that the employees of the Department of Diagnostic Laboratories suspend vacations and out-of-town travel for the next two weeks. Tell them to report immediately on any illness within the next two weeks. In the meantime, Police Inspector Rashid Siddiqi will continue questioning some employees of the department today and tomorrow. He will report to us, but we also will be talking to some of your employees. We would like to learn about the Institute, in general, and later we may inquire about details of your operation."

Mr. Clinton, dressed in a dark suit, white shirt, and a bright tie, was sitting at his desk with both a look of importance and concern. He said, "It is difficult to present the specifics of this institution in short terms. First of all, although its title includes 'Research Institute,' it is also an accredited hospital. We do accept some patients, currently about one hundred in-patients, but only those with some rare immunological disorders that other hospitals are not properly equipped to treat. The uniqueness of this institution is a very individualized approach to the patients based on their genetic and immunological make-up. This approach is based on results from the Human Genome Project completed some years ago and the subsequent developments of protocols for analyzing the DNA sequencing in patients, which represents a trend into medicine of the future. We have been and are continuing to develop tools to analyze a broad range of molecular testing that allows us to identify genetic deficiencies in each patient, and often incorporate this information into the specific therapy. That's why our Department of Diagnostic Laboratories is quite different from that in other hospitals — it includes genetic, molecular, and immunology laboratories.

"At the same time, we also have the regular diagnostic laboratories, including the Core Laboratory directed by Dr. David Brinkley, where standard lab tests are performed. Moreover, due to the growing TB problem in the world, we also have a reference tuberculosis laboratory directed by Dr. Henry Frontier, with unique tools to address this problem. Another large laboratory is the Microbiology/Virology Laboratory directed by Dr. Chuck Crowley.

Also, because of the costly research of the problems we are dealing with, we need substantial financial support in addition to the funding from the National Institutes of Health (NIH), from insurance companies paying for admitted patients, private donations, and other sources. In this regard, the revenue generated by our large Department of Diagnostic Laboratories, with more than a hundred employees, is very helpful. In fact, the revenue generated by this department, almost $150 million annually, not only pays for all the direct and indirect expenses of this department, but also contributes half of it to the general funds of the institution. You will learn more when visiting some of these laboratories, which may be helpful in your investigation."

"Mr. Clinton, as I understand, people present here are leaders of the Department of Diagnostic Laboratories. Would you introduce them to us?"

"Yes, of course. I apologize that I didn't do it at the beginning. This is Dr. Jim Dellinger, the Executive Director of the Department of Diagnostic Laboratories. This position was created two years ago to help us in dealing with finances and revenue, for compliance with the regulations, and especially for handling the lab reports for our patients here and the lab reports that are going out. The Director of Operations (Dr. Meyer was in this position) reports to the Executive Director. We valued very much the job done by Dr. Meyer, allowing him to have an additional job and even supporting his involvement in the local hockey team. These amenities often created some envy among other employees.

"We have here five directors of the individual laboratories: Dr. Michael Gilman, Pharmacology; Dr. Chuck Crowley, Microbiology; Dr. Henry Frontier, Tuberculosis); Dr. Bharat Gupta, Molecular Diagnostics; and Dr. Peter Vincent, Immunology. You will meet with some of them when visiting the laboratories. Also reporting to the Executive Director are some people who are not present here today, such as the Director of Regulatory and Compliance Department, Director of New Developments in collaboration with the industry, Director of Finances, Director of Marketing, and Supervisor of the Client Services Group. We have provided you with the whole administrative structure and names of all employees in the department. At this point, I suggest that all my colleagues go now to meet with their employees and the police inspector, while Dr. Dellinger and I continue explaining our operation to Mr. Powell and his colleagues."

After they left, Mr. Powell made a suggestion. "Mr. Clinton, as I understand, you have quite a complex system of management with so many directors and supervisors, and we are particularly interested in details of interaction among the employees, especially among those at the managerial level. Sometimes, some conflicting issues may go beyond the day-to-day business and involve some personal antagonism, depending of course, on the character of individuals involved. Would you address this issue, please?"

"Within this department, we have seven laboratories, each headed by a prominent scientist. They are faculty members of the Department of Medicine, and have a Ph.D. degree. Drs. Frontier and Crowley also hold an M.D. and a 'professor' title. The main goal of these directors is to conduct research and development with publications that promote this institution. These scientists are top experts in their fields, and they systematically obtain grants from the NIH and pharmaceutical companies. From these grants, they hire some technicians to conduct the research experiments. These technicians do not report to the laboratory supervisors, which sometimes creates tension in interactions with other technicians conducting in the same area routine testing under pressure of intense scheduling and a lot of regulations. The laboratory directors' names attract many potential clients to submit specimens for complicated testing. Also, they provide general directions for the laboratories' operation. Recently, some were relieved from their involvement in the daily routine, which wasn't appreciated by everyone."

After a short break, Mr. Clinton continued, "The everyday operation of routine testing is conducted under direct supervision by a supervisor in each laboratory. This work is also subject to control by the Director of Operations and by the Director of the Regulatory and Compliance Department. So, each supervisor has at least three 'bosses,' which sometimes creates tension, especially when deviations from the approved protocol for each procedure are discovered by random visits from the Director of Regulation. It is necessary to have such a complex system to maintain a high level of accreditation by the College of American Pathologists (CAP), which conducts unannounced annual inspections. By the way, because this institution is accredited as a hospital, we are also inspected by the Joint Commission for Hospital Accreditation and by other agencies, all checking on compliance with various and ever-growing regulations. That is why we have a compliance department in charge of these issues. At least two laboratories, Microbiology and TB, are inspected by the security office and outside agencies to ensure that bio-safety regulations are observed. Constant pressure from these inspections, in addition to so many 'bosses,' is an unavoidable source of tension and conflicts, but I don't think it's the source of extreme hate that would lead to murder."

"Mr. Clinton, the list of laboratories you have provided includes seven laboratories, and I have a question about the Genetic Research Laboratory. How is it different from the diagnostic laboratories?"

"Yes, you are right, actually it is not a diagnostic laboratory, but for the convenience of administration it was put under the umbrella of this department, the director reports to the Executive Director only, and there is no interaction with the Director of Operations. This laboratory is conducting research related to creating some tissues that, in the future, can be used for transplantation, and is doing some stem-cell research funded by a pharmaceutical company. So far, we have kept a low profile with this work because, as you know, there are political issues around this problem. Again, Dr. Meyer was not connected with this work."

Mr. Powell had been showing some impatience with the presentation, and finally interjected, "I would like you to address any possible 'areas of tension' that we may encounter while speaking with the employees. Also, in general, what can you tell us about Dr. Meyer as a person?"

At this point, Dr. Dellinger interrupted the conversation between Clinton and Powell, and said, "First, I would like to address your question about Dr. Meyer. We hired him because of his special knowledge and training in management of the working environment, but at that time we did not have a Director of Operations position. Therefore, we appointed him as Associate Director in the Microbiology Laboratory, using the fact that he also was trained in microbiology. Only last year we were able to establish the Director of Operation position, which is necessary for my interaction with the laboratory supervisors in regard to the routine day-to-day operation. Dr. Meyer was a very handsome man, and you may hear rumors that some female employees were competing for his attention and, in particular, about his relationship with his administrative assistant. We have had no evidence of any wrongdoing or complaints to warrant any disciplinary action."

At this moment, Dr. Dellinger stood up, becoming the dominating center of attention of the group, not so much because of his title, but more so because of his distinctive appearance — very tall (about six-foot-seven) with broad shoulders and long black hair brushed to the back. In contrast to his appearance, Dr. Dellinger spoke in a high-pitched voice, which was not a surprise to his colleagues, but made the visitors turn their heads toward him. He said, "Now I would like to address something about myself, because you will hear about it anyway. I separated from my wife after she refused to move with me here from our previous residence in New Jersey, and I hope to get a formal divorce from her soon. Here, I met a lady whose name is Martha Trump; she used to be Supervisor of Client Services Group, mostly clerical people. We became involved, and I am planning to marry her after my divorce is settled. She was employed at this institution before I came to Greeneville. I didn't give her preferential treatment. Our relationship became public knowledge, so she resigned here and took another job at the State Department of Health. Related to this was a conflict with the previous Director of Marketing, Mr. Flaming, who once publically during a Directors' meeting insulted me, saying that I was a dishonorable person by cheating on my wife and having an affair with a subordinate. At the time of this incident, Martha was no longer employed here, and everybody knew what the actual situation was. A week before his verbal attack on me, I had reprimanded Mr. Flaming for improper activities at a scientific conference where he was handling a marketing booth for our institution. Perhaps he was attempting to protect himself from being fired by deflecting blame onto me. He was fired. A few other individuals were fired for various reasons, but I doubt that any of these events are related to Dr. Meyer's death."

Mr. Powell was not fully satisfied with the overview that was presented and continued with his questioning, but it was the end of the day, and Mr. Clinton suggested adjourning until the next morning.

"One more question—you mentioned a Directors' meeting. Tell me what the substance of these meetings is, and what is the usual interaction among your colleagues? Are there conflicts of the kind you described with Mr. Flaming?"

"Well, one situation that may be of interest is the weekly meetings that Dr. Meyer initiated after his appointment as Director of Operations. Initially, he requested attendance by all lab directors and supervisors. The directors resented Dr. Meyer's dominance, and some of them just avoided these meetings. That arrangement was changed, and only the supervisors participated, to discuss only the issues about the routine operation. Then we started having monthly meetings with the directors to address major issues, including new developments, interactions with the outside clients and industry, revenue and expenses, observance of regulations, and recruitment of new employees. Representatives from the Departments of Finance, Personnel, and Security usually attended."

The meeting was adjourned. The Institute's employees left earlier feeling on the spot and like they were subjects of suspicion; nothing good could be expected from police and FBI agents snooping around. Each of them went to their laboratories to prepare for the likely unpleasant visits.

Chapter 2 -

Investigation Begins

Gloria West was born and grew up in Berthoud, Colorado, a small town of fewer than 10,000 people. The town was surrounded by farmland, and often referred to as the 'Garden Spot of Colorado.' Gloria attended the only high school in town, and always dreamed of leaving Berthoud. The main reason was not so much the boring life in town, but her home life. Her father was a blacksmith, a firmly committed member of the local Presbyterian Church. The only peaceful moments during the day were when the family, including her two younger brothers, would gather for a meal and say the blessings. Beyond that, the family was constantly quarreling about anything and everything, which frequently resulted in angry and hateful words being spoken to each other. In general, it could be said that the family was dysfunctional. Being recognized by some of her friends as an attractive girl, Gloria decided she would move to another city after her graduation from high school. After finding an advertisement for a secretarial (administrative assistant) position in Greeneville, she applied for the job and traveled there, despite her parent's adamant opposition. She got the job, thanks to her good marks from school and a certificate for completing special secretarial classes.

Soon after arriving in Greeneville, Gloria met a young man who recently came to the U.S. with his parents from England. Gloria and Hans West got married and, in a year, Gloria gave birth to a baby girl. People in the department treated her very nicely, especially those new friends to whom she confessed about her unpleasant family experience. Gloria would often comment that she found a real family at work. The only obstacle to her happiness was the fact that she actually did not love her husband. Sometimes she could hardly tolerate him, especially on an intimate level. Sometimes just his touch irritated her so much to the point that at times she would leave their bed to sleep on the sofa, making excuses about not feeling well. Hans did not know how to arouse Gloria; much less master the finer points of lovemaking. He naively thought that trying different positions was the key, but instead he only succeeded in bringing himself to an orgasm before Gloria was even aroused. Sex was just not a subject of discussion among his friends back in his hometown of Perth in Scotland. Obviously, Hans was not an experienced lover, and he thought that Gloria was just a frigid woman, the type he had heard some people talk about. Eventually Hans lost interest in intimacy altogether. Perhaps, years later, Hans would meet another more experienced woman who would help him overcome the humiliating experience with Gloria.

Dr. Meyer, who had recently become Director of Operations, began paying some attention to Gloria. Now that he was Director of Operations, he was entitled to have an administrative assistant. Gloria applied for the position and got the job. Dr. Meyer was a married man, but that did not deter him from becoming involved with Gloria. The problem was keeping their involvement secret. Gloria was sublimely happy, for she had finally discovered the pleasure of sex, and what orgasm, often mentioned by her new friends, really meant. She would refer to Dr. Meyer as her boss and her friend, but not admitting even to her close friends the depth of their relationship.

Rashid Siddiqi, the police inspector, was questioning Mrs. Gloria West. "So you're the one who found the body, is that right, Mrs. West?"

"Yes, that's right. He was a very dear friend and, of course, I wanted to say goodbye. I hadn't seen him for two days—I had been at home with a cold. Today I only saw him at a distance and for a short time at the party and then he disappeared. Later on, I saw his car in the parking lot. The headlights were on and the motor running, and well, I...I came up to the car...and...and, well...." Gloria broke down into quiet sobs.

The inspector put his hand on her hand, trying to comfort her; a crying woman always unnerved him.

"Okay, okay, here's a tissue, Mrs. West. Try to keep yourself together."

She paused briefly, and then took the tissue from the inspector. After blowing her nose she managed to continue, "He was just... just *sitting* there, you know? He just looked so...*slack*."

"And that's when you called for help?" the inspector asked, maintaining eye contact.

She put her hand over her face to hide her tears. "Yes, yes."

The inspector paused while writing his notes. He thought a moment, and then continued with his questioning. "Now, do you know if Dr. Meyer had any history of illness, any chronic heart conditions, or any medical problems?"

"Oh, no, he was wonderfully fit. He didn't have any medical conditions that I know about. In fact, Derrick would go to the gym several times a week, even ate very healthily, from what I saw. He also played hockey, particularly today in the morning. He complained to someone of being tired when he came back, and had very little food at the party, and, perhaps, went to his car to rest. He was only thirty-eight, you know. Do you think it could have been a heart attack or something like that, officer?"

"Well, ma'am, if I've learned anything, it's that nothing is certain in the case of sudden death. It could have been anything from a heart attack to suicide, or even some kind of, eh...poisoning."

Gloria's big brown eyes opened wide and she took a small, clumsy step backwards. "So you think...you're saying that this could have been...," West took a moment to reorient herself, "you think that he was murdered?"

"As I said, nothing's certain. Was there anyone particularly close to Dr. Meyer with whom I might be able to speak?"

"Well, there is a woman. Rebecca Brown; she is a supervisor in the Microbiology Laboratory. Derrick used to work there as an Associate Director before his appointment to Director of Operations. They sometimes ate lunch together," West said meekly.

"Is that it? Was there anyone else close to him? Or anyone who worked with him, maybe someone who would've wanted him out of the way?"

"Oh, well…" Gloria thought for a moment, closing the lids on her deep, soft brown eyes, and then answered, "Dr. Meyer was overseeing the operation of all laboratories, including for a short period of time, the productivity and efficiency of the scientists working in the labs. Derrick was a meticulous and loyal company man, so he made many enemies within the department because of his tough managerial decisions over these scientists. They didn't like being told what to do, you see. He didn't trust some of those scientists; he always felt like they were trying to pull the wool over his eyes since he did not fully understand many of the procedures they were performing. Oh, poor Derrick, you don't think anyone in the Institute has anything to do with this, do you?"

"To be honest, ma'am, I haven't a clue."

"But you'll find out, won't you?"

"I'll certainly try." The inspector flipped the cover on his pocketsize notepad and slipped it with his pen in the inside breast pocket of his jacket. He looked up. "Okay, Mrs. West, you can go home and get some rest. We didn't put you in quarantine because you haven't been in close contact with Dr. Meyer for four days. You've had a difficult day, you must feel exhausted."

With that, the inspector turned his back, motioned to one of his assistants, and they began packing up their equipment.

The next day, Inspector Rashid Siddiqi was reviewing the facts from the Meyer case. The inspector was an elderly, light-skinned man, with wisps of white hair that spread across the top of his wrinkled forehead. He had an easygoing manner, with a quick, though harmless temper. He had a watchful eye, and was always thinking, observing, and calculating in the back of his mind.

As he was rereading the notes he had written while interviewing the pretty lady who had discovered Meyer's body, he thought she cried a bit too much. In his experience, those who had recently witnessed or experienced the death of friend, especially a close one, were too deep in shock to express any intense emotions. The usual reaction was one of utter disbelief.

As thoughts flickered through Siddiqi's calculating brain, a bright young rookie agent — with glasses, a strong, clean-shaven chin, and a military-style haircut — appeared at his side.

"So, what do you think? Homicide?" the young man inquired.

Siddiqi hated questions that he considered stupid. By training, he didn't like to say what he was thinking and, furthermore, nothing he could say now would be either justified or interesting.

From what he had gathered from several witnesses at the crime scene, Inspector Siddiqi had a few important house calls to make. Among them were two names that he'd circled, underlined, and highlighted in his notes — Dr. Michael Gilman, and Dr. Chuck Crowley. Rashid wanted to see if the doctors were available.

Saving the best for last, Siddiqi decided to stop by and ask Mrs. Brown a few questions.

Rebecca Brown became a supervisor after a number of years working as a technician in some of the laboratories at the institution. She grew up in a large loving family in Kansas City, with two brothers and three sisters. Despite the loving and pleasant environment, she always had a tendency to subdue her siblings, both older and younger than she. This behavior carried over into her relationship with her schoolmates and, as a result, Rebecca only had a few girlfriends. She made a habit of reporting to the teachers any perceived wrongdoings by her classmates, even by her friends. Some teachers liked her, some did not, but she was a good student and always received good grades. Rebecca's quest for dominance and control continued when she entered college. With a good record and high marks, she easily got the job at the Institute in Greeneville. She soon married Mark, a young man who worked as a nurse at the same institution. She and Mark knew each other from college and often met up at football games and other sporting events.

Rebecca was an avid sports fan, especially boxing, wrestling, and ultimate fighting. These inherently violent sports tended to exacerbate her already heightened libido. Often while observing sport competitions and even at some movies, extreme punches, bleeding, pain, injuries, and other signs of violence made her so excited that she would develop an accelerated heartbeat and become horny and wet, almost to the point of orgasm. In fact, Rebecca would become so sexually aroused while watching macho men inflict violence on each other, her only desire was to rush home and have sex. Before marrying Mark, masturbation was a frequent activity in which she engaged. Much to Rebecca's disappointment, Mark was unable to satisfy her insatiable sexual needs and, though it was handy to have him available for sex, she didn't hold him in high esteem.

Derrick's presence in the microbiology laboratory did not change her life very much, but she was immediately attracted to this handsome and strong blond-haired man. One Sunday when Mark was out of town visiting his parents in Denver, she invited Derrick to a boxing match. After the match, Rebecca invited him to her home for a drink. One could only imagine what happened there... Thereafter, she and Derrick began meeting for sexual rendezvous whenever Mark was away. Derrick was the lover Rebecca longed for; having sex with him was rough and possessive, just what she liked. He could give her multiple orgasms and she loved feeling him explode inside her. In spite of all this, there was a problem. After sex, Derrick would fall very soundly asleep, as if he were unconscious. Rebecca would become anxious when she had trouble waking him. She was not only unnerved by his deep sleep, but was worried that someone might come to visit and find him there.

Their trysts ended after he was appointed Director of Operations and became attracted to his secretary, Gloria. It was an understatement to say that Rebecca was livid and viewed Derrick's dalliance with Gloria as a personal betrayal. During her affair with Derrick, she had softened her behavior toward her subordinates in the laboratory, but she soon returned to her humiliating and domineering ways, often pinpointing insignificant infractions.

When a gentleman walking in the hallway outside her door was asked by the inspector if he knew where Mrs. Brown was, the young man offered that she might be found at a small café a block away. The inspector found Rebecca sitting alone at a small table. The young woman, immersed in a thick paperback novel, didn't notice the formidable man until he had already sat down in the chair across from her.

"Don't look so startled, pretty lady; I just want to ask you a few questions."

"Who are you?"

"Inspector Siddiqi."

"Oh, so you're here about Dr. Meyer?"

"Yes, that's right, Mrs. Brown. As I understand, you were very close with him. I'm sorry for what you must be going through."

"We knew each other pretty well, yes. Thanks for your concern, though."

"Yes."

"I assume you're going to ask me some questions, Inspector?"

"Now that you mention it — as I said, I do have a few questions I'd like to ask you, Mrs. Brown — eh, may I call you Rebecca?"

"Mrs. Brown is fine."

"Are you currently involved with anyone? I mean romantically, of course."

"Excuse me? I hardly see how this is police business, and if it's something else you're looking for — go look somewhere else." Rebecca abruptly pushed out her chair, swept her book into her handbag, and walked swiftly to the cashier to pay for her coffee. The inspector rose from the table and with his long strides, was directly behind her. Turning quickly without looking, Rebecca stumbled headlong into Siddiqi's solid body. He didn't budge an inch.

"Excuse me."

"Now listen, I have some serious questions to ask you. We believe that Dr. Meyer may have been murdered. It is of utmost importance that I have your statement."

"But what do I have to do with any of this? I don't understand. Please, I have some things to take care of at home."

"Like what—cleaning the dishes? Listen, Mrs. Brown, you don't want to become uncooperative. I'm speaking with you because you were mentioned in one of our witness statements."

"What? Ugh, *that woman*—"

"...What woman?"

"Well, I suppose you know anyway. Gloria West, that incompetent slut. And now she's giving me police trouble. Great!"

"What do you mean?"

"She was his administrative assistant. She and Dr. Meyer always went to lunch together, and then disappeared for hours on end. Gloria used to be late to work every single day. Dr. Meyer would open her office door, turn on her desk lamp, spread some papers, and turn on the computer; you know, to make it look like she was at work, but just away from her office."

"Thank you very much, Mrs. Brown; we may talk more later."

Disturbing thoughts from the conversation with the police inspector stayed in Rebecca's mind for a long time. They brought back memories of her relationship with Derrick that she never shared with anybody. It pained her to see him around, wondering about his relationships with another woman. She had even considered moving away and began looking for another job, but now with his sudden death....

Rashid realized that most of the employees had already left, but he needed to talk to few more people. First was Dr. Crowley, Director of the Microbiology/Virology Laboratory, and Rashid would visit him at home.

"Dr. Crowley?"

It took a while, but after a long series of knocks, Chuck Crowley finally opened the door.

"Inspector Rashid Siddiqi. May I come in?"

"Yeah, yeah sure. Grab a seat by the TV."

Crowley lived in a fairly upscale apartment in the newly developed downtown area of Greeneville. The place was nice — oak paneling on the walls, various exotic pictures, and expensive-looking paintings. Plush Persian carpets lay on the cherry wood floors. A kitchen, dining/living room area, bedroom, office, balcony, and two bathrooms completed the layout. Of course, the place wasn't particularly clean, but Rashid could hardly blame a bachelor that lived alone for not keeping a tidy apartment.

"So, let me see if I can guess a few things before you start with the questions. You're investigating Derrick Meyer's death, and you've heard that Dr. Meyer and I didn't quite get along, especially after he left my laboratory to become a big boss. Now, if what *I've* heard about you police officers is correct, you're all eager to see how this could be a murder case, and I'm your prime suspect?" All this was said with a smile and a kind of sarcasm.

"Okay, but let us be serious. What can you tell me about your laboratory and about Dr. Meyer that may be useful in our investigation?"

"My laboratory is well-known locally and beyond because we have developed quite sophisticated procedures to identify a broad range of viruses that cause flu and many other flu-like illnesses that create frequent outbreaks. This alone brings very substantial revenue from testing patients' specimens submitted to us from other hospitals and clinics. Meyer never learned proper performance of these procedures when he worked in this laboratory, and never appreciated their importance. After all, he was not so much a microbiologist, but rather a full-scale bureaucrat, despite his Ph.D. degree. His behavior, as well as his physical appearance changed after he became Director of Operations. He started having weekly meetings with the laboratory supervisors, and even requested that lab directors attend, to which we strongly objected and eventually our attendance at these meetings was no longer requested. It was a way to assert his administrative power and dominance.

Dr. Meyer was a man who lived in the present, but seemed to identify more with the 1950s. He subtly projected the 'bad boy image,' reminiscent of the teenage boys in the 1956 film *Blackboard Jungle*. The boys in the film were sullen, always spoiling for a rumble; they would sneer at the teacher and derisively call him 'teach' or 'daddy-o.' But, in his new position, Derrick maintained the proper decorum, yet, he still displayed some 'bad boy' characteristics. His primary goal was to intimidate people around him, which he managed to do in a variety of ways. For example, to make everyone aware of his presence, he walked with an arrogant swagger, purposely hitting the cleats on his loafers loud enough for all to hear. And to elevate himself literally and figuratively above the rest of the group, he would sit on a table with his feet on a chair or would perch on the back of the chair.

"Well, but what was, in your opinion, the perception of him by others?"

"Other professionals around him did not trust him and this became the source of negative feelings toward Dr. Meyer, not only by me, but by others, as well. To understand our feelings on this issue, you can talk to Dr. Filatov, who came from Russia and worked for a while with Dr. Meyer in the microbiology laboratory. In private conversation, he often referred to Dr. Meyer as 'Commissar.' He used to explain the origin and meaning of this term. The story was that Vladimir Lenin, the founder of the Soviet Union, once said, 'With the new regime (Soviet Union) we will replace all the 'experts' inherited from the capitalist system with workers, and the housewives will run our country.' And, so they did, which resulted in the fall of the Soviet Union in 1991. The question is: What will happen to such fields as science, medical care, and economy in the U.S. if these important areas of our lives are dominated by the modern-day 'Commissars'? It is not rare that some modern-day 'Commissars' declare that they are able to quickly learn the specifics of an operation without the involvement of experts in the decision-making process in the field under question, thus, expediting an executive decision."

"That is a very interesting story, and maybe I will have a chance to hear it again directly from Dr. Filatov."

"Anyway, Derrick's bureaucratic skills were highly appreciated by the administration and were used to put some pressure on us, the laboratory directors. Beyond that, I cannot imagine anything that may be related to his death."

The next visit was to Dr. Michael Gilman, Director of the Pharmacology Laboratory. After a pair of knocks, a light-haired woman opened the door to Dr. Gilman's home.

"Hello, Mrs. Gilman, is your husband at home?"

"Eh...hello...good afternoon. Who is asking?" the woman replied, speaking with a noticeable Russian accent.

Siddiqi briefly explained that he was a police inspector, and he needed to ask Dr. Gilman some questions. All the while, the woman at the front door appraised him with questioning eyes, perhaps trying to determine if he indeed was who he said he was. He decided that she was a clever and cautious woman. A man, he thought, is lucky to have such a wife. She reminded him of many women he had known growing up in Pakistan and Jordan. There, it had been an absolute necessity for a woman to be cautious, because she was in constant danger at the hands of the unaccounted for criminal population, and the sex-deprived adolescents who were prone to abducting young women.

Finally, there appeared at the door a clean-cut man in his mid-thirties, nearly six-feet tall with dark hair. He had a curious, yet friendly, expression.

"Dr. Gilman?"

"Oh, yes, we met yesterday. Please come in."

Gilman had been on edge for the past couple of days since the police investigation had begun. For him, it had started with some unnecessary questioning about his lab activities, particularly those involving Dr. Derrick Meyer. It was unusual for such a young man to suddenly die, Michael admitted to himself, but it seemed as though the police department was making this out to be a murder. From Gilman's point of view, this was illogical. These sorts of things happened all the time—unpredictable heart attacks, brain aneurysms, or even deadly shock due to any number of medical conditions. Moreover, Derrick Meyer was a man working in a professional environment. His colleagues, and, in fact, most of the people he knew were professionals. Few such people commit murder in the real world. In the minds of action-hungry, bored-out-of-their-minds police inspectors, however, a potential murderer was lurking behind every oak tree, street lamp, and barbeque grill in and around the town.

"Dr. Gillman, may I ask you to tell me briefly about your laboratory and anything about Dr. Meyer that may be helpful in our investigation?"

"The primary function of my laboratory is to determine drug concentrations in patients' blood to help doctors adjust proper dosing of medications to achieve the optimal effect, on one hand, and to avoid potential side effects, on the other. Also, we give recommendations on how to handle inevitable side effects of these drugs. In connection with these tasks, we are also developing new procedures for determining the drugs' blood concentrations, which requires excellent skills and knowledge by those who work in my laboratory. Unfortunately, Dr. Meyer did not understand the complexity of this work beyond the issues of expenses and revenue, which was often the source of conflict with him.

"A few months back, I needed an extra technician in my lab to keep up with the volume of work we were getting. The procedures we perform take *time*, and I needed help in preparing the samples and programming the machines. It entails more than just setting some beakers over a Bunsen burner and waiting, as he seemed to think. So, I went to Meyer with my request. Now don't ask me why, but you see at some point the Institute decided that we *professionals*, even the professors, needed some busy-body 'managers' to keep an eye on us, to make sure we weren't spending too much. Well, these nobodies get paid the same as me, only they don't seem to do much except say 'no.' So when I requested an extra technician, of course, Meyer said, 'No.'"

"Then what?"

"Let me tell you a story from literature to illustrate the situation. George Bernard Shaw wrote the following in his famous play, *The*

Doctor's Dilemma: 'Mere experience is by itself nothing. If I take my dog to the bedside with me, he sees what I see. But he learns nothing from it. Why? Because he is not a scientific dog.' Dr. Meyer decided to spend some time in my laboratory to find out whether my request was justifiable. According to the account given by Gordon, a technician in the laboratory, he sat, watched, and recorded the time needed for Gordon to perform each step of the laboratory procedure. With a great sense of humor Gordon told me later, 'He was so under-educated about the procedures I was doing, that if I had wanted, I could have shown him any timing. He was too ignorant and had no clue as to what I was doing.' So, he saw everything that Gordon did, but learned nothing. Why? Because he is not a 'scientific dog.'

"And, it's true that I didn't like him much. He was under-qualified, overpaid, and a damned nuisance — uh, respectfully speaking, of course; I mean no disrespect to the deceased. I really hated this guy; I mean, this guy, who hadn't ever set a foot in medical school, is telling me how many people I do or do not need in my lab, and he was making me beg for help! Anyway, he finally agreed to it, but not until he had done some 'observation' in my lab. All in all, the process took about three weeks. All that, then he was constantly trying to take money out of the grants I was bringing in. These grants were strictly my territory — research. But he would say, 'Oh, but look at this grant; this is not for research, it is only for testing,' and he would try to dip his fingers into it. That is all that I can tell you about Dr. Meyer — perhaps, not very helpful for your investigation?"

Upstairs in the detective's wing of the police department, Rashid Siddiqi was showing his notes to Mr. Powell and two other FBI agents.

"*So...* what do you see?"

"Well, the way it looks, this guy Derrick Meyer was a real douche bag. I knew a whole bunch just like him back when I was working as an assistant at that big law firm. I can imagine he'd made some real enemies in the professional sector at that institute."

"Got that. What do you make of the witnesses?"

"Hmm. There's definitely catfight going on between Mrs. West and Mrs. Brown. Gloria's the pretty one of the two, am I right?"

"Go on."

"My guess is that Meyer was playing the two of them, had them competing for his attention, only it sounds like Mrs. West was winning. Either way, I think Mrs. Brown found out about it, and who knows, maybe she got angry, took some samples from the lab, slipped them in his drink at the barbeque…and boom! You've got a homicide."

"And say it was homicide. Are you ruling out Mrs. West?"

"Well, yeah, it's obvious. Not only was she winning the competition, but hell, she's got nothing to be sore about. "

"Well, you've gathered some interesting information. Thanks for your help. We'll take it over from here. I'll contact you again if we need your further help. Now, let's make further plans to interview employees of this department and visit some laboratories, but I want you, Mr. Siddiqi, to be informed about our activities here and any information we may obtain.

"We have to give special attention to the Microbiology and Tuberculosis laboratories as potential sources of infection to Dr. Meyer. Jim, I want you to visit the TB Laboratory, while you, Clare, should visit the Microbiology Laboratory and particularly speak to Dr. Filatov, who as an outsider may provide some additional information about the interactions between Dr. Meyer and others when he worked in that laboratory. Don't ask him direct questions about the people in the lab. He will provide this information anyway. Just try to divert his attention to your interest in his experience back in Russia. I'll talk to Mrs. Meyer, and get acquainted with the Immunology and Molecular Diagnostics Laboratory. Let's complete these interviews as soon as possible, before we get any results from the CDC. It may take some time until they have any conclusive results, especially if the results are negative. They submitted specimens to other agencies for expedited testing, such as the FBI's Hazardous Material Response Unit, U.S. Army Medical Research Institute of Infectious Diseases (USAMRIID) in Fort Detrick, Maryland, and Armed Forces

Institute of Pathology (AFIP). Also, they'll send a sample to the Genetic Research Laboratory at this institute after they are able to guarantee that it's not infectious. So, perhaps we will be involved in this case for some time.

Chapter 3 -

In the Microbiology Lab

The Microbiology/Virology and Tuberculosis laboratories were located in the right and left wings on the top floor of the seven-story building. The directors' offices were adjacent to the laboratories. Both laboratories were designed for Bio-Safety Level 3 practices (BSL-3), but visitors could meet the directors without going through the tedious procedure required for entry into the laboratory. The FBI agents, Jim Galen and Clare Whitcomb, met on the seventh floor. Agent Galen went to Dr. Henry Frontier's office, and Agent Whitcomb proceeded to Dr. Chuck Crowley's office.

Clare Whitcomb knocked on Dr. Crowley's door and, after a few moments, his assistant opened the door. "I'm Agent Whitcomb; I'm here to see Dr. Crowley."

From his inner office, Dr. Crowley could hear the exchange between his assistant and Agent Whitcomb, whereupon he immediately opened his door. In his usual gracious manner, Crowley smiled broadly and said, "Come in, come in; have a seat."

With an outstretched arm, he motioned toward a chair in front of his desk. At the age of seventy, Dr. Crowley had taken this current job as a pleasant alternative to retirement from his previous job at Columbia University. He was still in good physical condition, although he was becoming quite bold and developing a belly. Throughout his life, he developed some fatherly manners when talking with people much younger than he, especially women. The scent of Chanel #5 whispered a sweet memory from long ago. Even though the doctor was at an advanced age and a bachelor, he still had an eye for beautiful young women. Agent Clare Whitcomb was his type of woman; she had strong features, dark eyes, her thick dark hair was styled in a short bob, and she wore minimal makeup. Her tailored business suit subtly revealed her slender well-proportioned figure. Crowley imagined that she was very athletic, maybe a hiker. He was intrigued. He complimented her on performing the important, and perhaps tough, job as an FBI agent, while remaining feminine and attractive. Clare was not impressed, as she was used to such reactions to her appearance.

"How can I help you, Ms. Whitcomb? I am sorry, is it Ms. or Mrs.?"

"It is Ms., but you may call me Clare. My visit to your laboratory is related to the fact that Dr. Meyer worked here before his appointment as Director of Operations for the department, and maybe I can learn something about his interactions with his colleagues. But first, may I ask you to describe the operation of your laboratory?"

"As I've explained previously to the police inspector, our main goal is to provide bacteriological diagnosis by testing patients' specimens. Unlike the standard microbiology laboratories at most of the state health departments, we have a virology section to diagnose a variety of viral infections, including those causing respiratory flu-like illnesses, HIV, etc. Also, we determine the drug-susceptibility of the bacterial and viral isolates to a broad range of drugs. This helps the doctors in choosing the right medications for treatment of their patients. All of this work requires sophisticated procedures, including molecular biology-based methods."

"What was Dr. Meyer's involvement in this operation when he worked in this laboratory?"

"He helped me and the laboratory supervisor to coordinate the testing, which often looks like an assembly line. He was especially helpful in setting up the drug-susceptibility procedures."

"What can you tell me about his relationship with others, in particular his relationship with Mrs. Brown, the laboratory supervisor?"

"My impression is that they had developed a friendship, and the morale in the laboratory was rather positive."

"Is it still 'positive' since Dr. Meyer left?"

"Well, it's hard to tell. There have been some changes within the last two years. The laboratory has expanded, with several new technicians joining the lab and, most importantly, I've received grants from the NIH and a pharmaceutical company to conduct research on the development and evaluation of new anti-viral antibiotics. With the money from these grants, I hired a scientist, Dr. Filatov, and two technicians. This group reports only to me, and is not involved in the general operation of the laboratory. This arrangement seems to have caused tension among the laboratory technicians. And, I should say, the laboratory supervisor Mrs. Rebecca Brown is very unhappy because she has no control over my research group. Dr. Meyer was also unhappy with this situation when he became the Director of Operations."

"May I have a look at the place where Dr. Meyer used to work?"

"Of course, Dr. Filatov occupies his office now, which is inside the laboratory. Before entering the laboratory, you'll have to put on some protective gear. Becky will assist you with that."

Rebecca showed Clare Whitcomb to the dressing room at the laboratory entrance and provided her with shoe covers, a disposable lab coat, sleeves, gloves, and a respirator. After Agent Whitcomb donned the protective gear, Rebecca gave a short tour of the laboratory, pointing out the five BSL-3 units that extended beyond the open bench area.

"There is an anteroom for each BSL-3 unit that is equipped with a device that monitors the air exchange and negative air pressure within the room itself," explained Rebecca. Clare could see that inside each room a technician wearing protective gear was working in front of the isolation hood. Agent Whitcomb was allowed to enter an anteroom only.

"May I see the place where Dr. Meyer used to work?"

"Of course, it is occupied now by Dr. Filatov. Let me introduce you to him."

They entered the office, and after the introduction, Rebecca left. Dr. Filatov and Ms. Whitcomb were left alone, but Clare felt that the situation was not conducive to addressing sensitive questions. She asked, "Dr. Filatov, is it possible to meet you someplace other than here? I have a few questions to ask?"

"I am busy now finishing some experiments, but I will be finished here in two or three hours and can meet you at the cafeteria near the park, if that suits you."

The warm weather and a slight breeze attracted many people to the outside dining area at lunchtime. Boris Filatov found a somewhat secluded table in the shade of a large oak tree. He expected Agent Whitcomb to arrive shortly, so he decided to go ahead and order a turkey sandwich and tea. Boris was seemingly aware of the attention he drew from onlookers. He was used to the stares and murmuring, though, for Dr. Filatov was an extraordinarily handsome man, almost seven feet tall, with broad shoulders. Even more striking was his long hair combed back and his mesmerizing deep blue eyes. Men envied him and women swooned over him.

More than forty minutes passed before Ms. Whitcomb arrived.

"I'm sorry for being late and I'm starving! Let me first order a turkey sandwich and a drink, and then we can talk."

Boris decided he was still hungry and, besides, he thought it would be awkward for her to eat alone, so he ordered more tea and another sandwich. Not much conversation took place while they ate, mostly just small talk.

"May I call you Boris? Please call me Clare."

"Yes, of course. I am used to that now, but some years ago, when I first came to the U.S., such familiarity was very unusual for me, especially in relationships between people of different ages, positions, and titles."

"Do you like your job? How is it compared to other places you've worked in the U.S.?"

"I came to the U.S. ten years ago, after being accepted to a post-doctoral program in molecular biology at Stanford University in California. Those three years of fellowship were a culmination of my lifetime experience in both research and a new life in the U.S. After a couple more years at that magnificent place, I decided to pursue the opportunity to live in the U.S. and not return to Russia," he said, smiling, but the deep blue eyes were reflective.

Ms. Whitcomb was curious, but instinctively knew that silence was in order. Presently, Boris continued his story. "My training back in Russia was in genetics of viruses, and my father, a prominent scientist in this field, thought that some experience in America would be beneficial for me. So, he used his connections and arranged for my trip to the U.S. Unfortunately, after my fellowship at Stanford, I could not find a job in this field that would support me remaining in the U.S.

"I had to make some compromises. I learned that a job in a commercial diagnostic laboratory would provide me with an opportunity to obtain U.S. residency and, subsequently, U.S. citizenship. According to the contract, I had to remain in that job for three years. I was well compensated, but I did not like the job, and the conditions there were very similar to those in Russia. Employees in the lab referred to it as a 'sweat shop.' The atmosphere was very formal and focused on revenue. I was surprised that neither a scientist nor a laboratory expert was in charge of the operation and making important decisions regarding the choice of technology used and tests to perform. I learned that all these decisions were handled by the Chief Financial Officer (CFO), an undereducated person whose only skill was manipulating the finances. Even the President of the 'Company' would not make even a small decision, without consulting with the CFO. Based on rumors circulated there, I was not surprised to learn that besides the official business, the CFO's power may have been related to his control and management of some tricky 'distributions' of funds/bonuses within the leadership. The most depressing fact was that there was no incentive or encouragement toward creativity beyond performing the approved routine procedures to generate the highest possible revenue."

"But, Boris, these commercial laboratories are business enterprises typical of capitalism, which is what you are favoring vs. socialism. What is your preference, after all?"

"I believe that commercialization of the laboratory services has merits, but to a certain point. An example of providing proper balance between the economical part of it and patient care is this institute. I am so glad that I got a job at this magnificent institution, but still not in the field that I am most interested in — molecular biology and genetics. They hired me because of my training in these areas, and promised to use me in these fields in the future. In the meantime, I was appointed to the Microbiology Laboratory to work in research and also to help with the virology issues. Being employed here is a very pleasant change, and I really enjoy it. Dr. Crowley is a great scientist and a very pleasant person, and working under his direction is an honor and a pleasure. Three of us in the research group work very hard, frequently working past normal hours, and often on weekends and evenings. Such an unusual setting sometimes creates envy among the laboratory technicians who must adhere to a strict schedule from eight-thirty A.M. to five P.M., with rigid scheduled breaks. I hope to eventually get another job in the Genetics Research Laboratory at this institution. I hope this information may help you in your investigation."

A few minutes of silence followed Boris's somehow emotional speech, after which he renewed the conversation. "Do you think that Dr. Meyer was killed? I hope that I am not a suspect?" he said in a kind of sarcastic and humorous tone.

"Oh, Boris, we don't know, yet, about Dr. Meyer's death; everybody is a suspect as long as the cause of death is unknown. I wanted to talk to you because you aren't directly involved with the department's operation and, as such, you may have a different perspective. At the same time, I'm genuinely interested in your experience, especially compared with that in Russia. In college, I took classes in history, psychology, and political science, and I'm still interested in these fields. I didn't finish college, instead I went to the Police Academy, but I am planning to go back someday to complete my education. Now, may I ask you some specific questions? You mentioned that Dr. Crowley is a pleasant person. How does he convey that in his management of the laboratory?"

"During the last year, Dr. Crowley hasn't been directly involved with the day-to-day operation of the lab. Responsibility for that was passed to the laboratory supervisor and Director of Operations. However, Dr. Crowley conducts weekly meetings with the technicians, where he reviews overall problems, provides advice on resolving any difficulties, addresses unusual cases, and updates them on any new developments in the field. He treats all the employees with the highest personal respect, referring to them as 'colleagues,' emphasizing that he considers them professionals. As such, in his opinion, everyone deserves the trust that he or she will accomplish the job without strict supervision and scheduling. The technicians like that sort of freedom, but the supervisor does not. Mrs. West has a very different management style and she's vigorously pursuing her desire for total control in all areas; in other words, she epitomizes micromanagement to the fullest."

After a pause, Boris said, "I'm sure you can see that this situation, along with the increasing volume of work, would create tension and conflicts. In the background, the relationship between Mrs. West and Dr. Meyer, with his frequent visits to the laboratory, recently was not very cordial, to say the least."

In a matter-of-fact tone, Ms. Whitcomb said, "You know, Dr. Filatov, as you've said, 'not very cordial,' isn't very specific. Can you elaborate in more detail? We are investigating a potential murder, and we're highly interested in the interactions among the people here."

With her pen poised, ready to make notes, she looked steadily into Boris's blue eyes. Nevertheless, Filatov took his time. Finally, Boris spoke. His reply was circumspect. After all, life had taught him the perils of speaking without due consideration of possible consequences.

"The difference in the relationship between Dr. Meyer and Mrs. West, when he was working here and then after he became Director of Operations, was quite dramatic. It went from friendship to hostility.

Everyone in the laboratory noticed that they often had heated arguments. Sometimes they could be heard screaming at each other. I, too, sensed the hatred Mrs. West had for Dr. Meyer whenever she referred to his suggestions. She would suddenly become extremely critical about the dual management, both professional under the laboratory directorship and bureaucratic with directions from Dr. Meyer. In this regard, she even referred to some of my stories about the inefficient dual system in the former Soviet Union."

"Oh, I am very interested in this, though it may be not directly related to my investigation. Can you describe this dual system of the Soviet Union more specifically?" Clare asked, leaning forward.

"Okay, but it will take some time, because I will have to address the historic roots of the Soviet bureaucracy. It is related to the early development of both military and civilian structures. Before WWII the structure of the Red Army, as the Soviet military was called, reflected the leadership's distrust of the professional military caste, a distrust that extended to nearly all professional groups. They devised a system where two individuals were in charge of every military unit, a military commander and a political commissar, the latter appointed by the Communist Party to monitor the commander. When the war started and the German armies began their rapid advance, the tension between commanders and commissars had a paralyzing effect when it came to making crucial decisions. For example, when the military commander saw the need to retreat in order to save the troops, the commissar, bound by the party line against retreats ('Not a step back!') would refuse to sign the order. Early in 1943 that all changed. The commissars then became 'political assistants' and the commanders had the full combatant authority restored. The course of the war started to change in favor of the Red Army, and the restored power of the military professionals greatly contributed to the victorious path."

"You are often using the term 'Commissar.' What exactly does that mean?"

"The term 'Commissar' denoted a politically motivated person with excessive administrative power. After the war, it became a word of the past, but no lessons resulted from that tragic war experience and the role of the commissars. The Communist Party control became an unpleasant fact, even more so than it was before or during the war.

"In the early years of the Soviet Union, 'Commissar' was widely used to emphasize the difference between the new system and the old pre-revolutionary system. For example, instead of 'Minister' the great positions were 'People's Commissar of Industry,' 'People's Commissar of Health Care,' 'People's Commissar of Foreign Affairs,' and so on. Decades later, when the title 'Commissar' became unpopular, it became 'Minister.' During the time of the commissars, there was enhanced control by the Communist Party of every activity. Every ministry, factory, university, high school, hospital, and scientific institution had a Communist Party Bureau, and the head of the Bureau, called the 'Secretary' or 'Part Org' for Party Organizer, had the same power as the commissar in the army at the beginning of the war. The Party Secretary of any department reported to the next level Secretary, who in turn reported to the Secretary of the district or the city bureau, and all the way up to the 'General Secretary,' who either was above the Soviet Prime Minister or occupied both posts. The actual head of the government, called Secretary of the Central Committee of the Communist Party, did not have to be a professional, and his expertise in any field was attributed to his high political wisdom. Stalin, Khrushchev, and Brezhnev all held this position during their rule. Not only did they lack professional education, but they also were nearly illiterate.

"This suffocating dominance by the Party caused stagnation in the economy and failure in nearly all fields of endeavor. This finally resulted in the disintegration of the Soviet Union in 1991! It was a big surprise for me to learn that parallel management also exists in the U.S., especially in nonprofit organizations. Here, too, similar to the Soviet Union, this bureaucracy grew out of mistrust of professionals by administrative leaders. In the U.S., managers play the role of commissars. These managers oversee the professionals (research scientists, for example), handling the financial aspects of their work, hiring, and firing of their employees, and other administrative tasks. It's not unusual for a laboratory 'director,' generally a professor with a Ph.D., to report to an administrative person with the title of manager or 'Department Director.' This individual, who usually lacks professional expertise, reports to an administrative executive rather than to the senior scientist. Sometimes when Mrs. West complained about Dr. Meyer's behavior, I jokingly called him 'commissar,' expressing some sympathy just to calm her down. In fact, I personally did not have any interaction with Dr. Meyer, nor did I develop an opinion about him."

"Thank you, Boris. Your explanation was very interesting, and thanks for sharing your story about the Soviet Union."

She hesitated, and then said, "Unfortunately, I have to go back to work now, but I would like to learn more about the history of the Soviet Union, and particularly your personal story, which I'm told is fascinating." They rose from their chairs and Clare asked Boris, "Would you be willing to talk with me again sometime about both the current situation and about your experience?"

"Of course, just give me a call." Boris handed her his business card.

Clare slipped the card in her tan leather messenger bag and extended her hand. Boris was impressed with her gentle, yet firm, handshake. She smiled and said, "Thanks again, Boris."

Boris watched her walk away. He sat down again under the old oak tree. Before returning to the distraction in the lab, he needed time to ponder the conversation that just transpired with Agent Whitcomb. He was puzzled. *Why does she really want to talk with me again?* He wondered. *Is she sincerely interested in my life in Russia, or is there another motive? Time will tell.*

Clare went back to her office to document her interview with Boris and other tasks. She then went home completely exhausted after the busy day. Her conversation with Boris revived her interest in history, but she also found herself thinking non-stop about this man with the stunning blue eyes, his delicate manners, and even his slight accent that softly punctuated perfectly spoken English. She went to bed still hearing Boris's voice in her head. She asked herself, "Am I becoming attracted to this man?" She decided to find an excuse to see him again.

At the same time, she realized that it would be impossible to pursue a possible relationship with him as long as she was involved in the investigation at the institute where he was an employee. But serendipity intervened at the symphony concert over the weekend. Boris spotted Clare during intermission and invited her for dinner after the concert, to which she readily accepted.

It was a pleasant occasion for both, but they didn't engage in deep conversation. Rather, they eagerly discussed Tchaikovsky's *Sixth Symphony*, which was a part of the program. Obviously, the beauty and passion of the music enraptured Boris and Clare.

"Boris, I feel that this dramatic music is filled with expressions of suffering, but also with an underlying current of hope. I was impressed with the sudden changes in mood, from slow soulful melody at the beginning, to a kind of a waltz in the middle, followed by a restless march, and ending with a peaceful resignation. It sounded very personal. Do you know the back story?"

"Tchaikovsky composed the *Sixth Symphony* in 1893 and conducted the premiere nine days before his death. He viewed this symphony as his most important accomplishment. Originally, it had the name *Pathétique* from the French, meaning in Russian 'passionate' or 'emotional,' but later this title has not been always used, and there were many speculations about the possible program behind it. Perhaps, you know that Tchaikovsky was a homosexual, he was trying to overcome his sexual attitude, and he considered himself possessed by devil. He even got married, but it was a short-lasting disaster. The music definitely reflects his suffering from controversies surrounding his life, and deals with the issues of life and death. Homosexuality was a crime in Russia at that time, and even later, in the Soviet Union. Nevertheless, many individuals in the upper classes, even in the Tsar's court, were involved in homosexual relationships, without any punishment, as long as there wasn't a scandal. Tchaikovsky's homosexuality was known, as was his brutal behavior with young boys that were provided to him by his butler. This was not a big secret. The situation changed when he got involved with a nephew of a high-ranking aristocrat, who was a close personal friend of the Tsar. To avoid humiliation in the court and subsequent exile to Siberia, Tchaikovsky was ordered to commit suicide. He poisoned himself with arsenic. The symptoms of arsenic poisoning are similar to cholera, so cholera was the officially stated as cause of death. The facts surrounding Tchaikovsky's homosexuality and the mystery of his death were forbidden topics in the Soviet Union. However, they came to light after the disintegration of the Soviet Union. Regardless of the views of Tchaikovsky as a person, he was one of the greatest composers, and he was a musical genius. I do admire most of his music."

"I would like to learn about Tchaikovsky. What would you recommend that I read?"

"I believe that the best biography of Tchaikovsky was published in 1996 by the famous British historian Anthony Holden. I have the book, and can give it to you."

At the end of the evening Clare and Boris realized that both of them had tickets to the next concert. Boris said he would bring the book then, which provided a good excuse to meet again…

Chapter 4 -

A Day in the TB Lab

D r. Henry Frontier, Director of the TB Laboratory, the largest within the Department of Diagnostic Laboratories, arrived at the lab at eight A.M. Beginning his day at this time, was a part of the routine within his strongly disciplined schedule. At the age of seventy-two, he was often complimented for looking much younger than his age. His fast and brisk movements, his slim and muscular body, and gray hair only around his temples, made people forget about his age. Being in perfect health as a former mountain climber, he did not have any plans for retirement and enjoyed the active research, as well the busy routine laboratory activities. Added to this was Dr. Frontier's national and international reputation and recognition as one of the top TB experts in the world, and his name was skillfully used by the Institute's administration for obtaining research grants from the NIH and industry, as well as for attracting referral services resulting in growing revenue.

He had just started his usual morning routine when a visitor appeared at his office door. The young man was, perhaps, in his early thirties with a noticeably athletic appearance. His very dark hair and dark eyes made him look much thinner than he actually was.

Without apology for his sudden appearance, the visitor said, "Dr. Frontier, I saw you yesterday at the general meeting with the investigating team. My name is Jim Galen, but please just call me

Jim. I am a member of the FBI team investigating Dr. Meyer's death; I have been assigned to familiarize myself with the operation of your laboratory. Each one of our team will do the same in the other laboratories."

Dr. Frontier stood up from his chair to shake hands with the visitor. "Please come in; sit down and make yourself comfortable. I understand the difficulties your team is facing in the investigation of Dr. Meyer's mysterious death. Perhaps, it is a good idea to learn about our operation, which may show you its complexity, as well as the related usual and sometimes not so usual interactions among people conducting quite sophisticated routine work."

Galen smiled in response while continuing to stare into Dr. Frontier's eyes.

"Yes, Doctor, I appreciate your help. How would you advise me to proceed?"

"You know, Jim, if you have enough time, I would recommend you to start right here at my office. Just take a seat at that table in the corner with your laptop and watch what happens today. I will explain to you the technical details of what is happening. I would like to review your notes with you for accuracy, and let's call your findings 'A Day in the Lab Director's Office.'

The day was quite busy from the very start. First, the Director's Assistant, John Meager, came with disturbing news that a shipment containing supplies sent by the Hain Life Science Company in Germany had been held up by the FDA because the diagnostic test for which the supplies were intended was not among the FDA-approved laboratory tests. In addition, John said the FDA required a letter stating that the test for which the supplies were to be used was for research purposes only, and not for diagnostic testing of patients' specimens. Only then would the shipment be released. Dr. Frontier signed the letter John had prepared, and now he faced the difficult task of explaining the situation to Jim Galen, who was already giving Dr. Frontier impatient looks.

"This situation is quite complex, and to understand it I will have to give you a short lecture, if we are not interrupted, about the current situation with tuberculosis."

With that, Jim expressed his eagerness to learn, and Dr. Frontier went to the blackboard to illustrate his explanations.

"First of all, you have to realize that tuberculosis is not a problem of the past, as it is often perceived by the public, but rather it is one of the most neglected world health problems of today," stated Dr. Frontier. "It kills almost two million people in the world annually, or one person every twenty seconds."

Jim impatiently interrupted, "I am really surprised by these numbers, because I thought that TB was a curable disease, and the question is: Why are so many people still dying from TB? I thought that the main killer in the world was AIDS, not TB. I just read an article recently published in *The Wall Street Journal* that in 2011 about 1.7 million people died from AIDS and about 2.5 million were infected with HIV."

"Your perception is not unique, but in this statistic many people recorded as having died from AIDS had both infections, HIV and TB, but the immediate cause of death was TB. Often the reported number of deaths from TB includes only those who died from TB *without* AIDS. Many people, even medical professionals, think that the major health problem among the infectious diseases of today is AIDS. It is primarily because AIDS is, indeed, a major problem in the U.S. and other industrialized countries, but the actual number of deaths from TB in the world, including those who also had AIDS, is greater than of those from AIDS, leprosy, and malaria combined. The deadliest health problem in countries with high TB prevalence is the combination of both infections, TB and AIDS. People infected with HIV, even before they develop AIDS, are highly susceptible to TB because of their very low level of immunity, and they usually develop a very severe and difficult to treat form of tuberculosis.

"You do have a reasonable perception that TB is a curable disease. There are at least twelve drugs that have been developed to treat this disease, but only some of these drugs are available in countries with the highest incidences of TB, such as India, China, and African countries. In addition to this, the greatest problem of today is the improper use of the limited number of drugs in these countries, the wrong combination of the drugs administered to the patients, or not a long enough period of treatment, often much less than the required minimum of six months. As a result, the tubercle bacilli in the patient's body become resistant to the administered drugs, making it difficult to treat such a patient, who then becomes a source to those around him of infection with drug-resistant bacteria. Many patients with drug-resistant TB are often completely incurable because their bacteria are resistant to almost all or even to all drugs. Some of these patients come to the U.S., and are undetected among the more than 40 million annual visitors. These visitors represent a source of infection with these dangerous bacteria to the general population."

"But, Doctor, don't we have specific regulations from the Center for Disease Control and Prevention (CDC) and specific regulations in each state to control the importation of infectious diseases, including tuberculosis?"

"Yes, Jim. We have many regulations and restrictions at all levels of administration. With regard to TB, according to these standards, anyone applying for immigration to the U.S. has an obligation to present his/her country's documentation on their health to the U.S. Embassy, including data on testing for TB. The problem is, there is no program or regulation regarding checking for TB, not among immigrants, but among visitors, many of whom are not just here short-term, but people such as students admitted to our universities who come to the U.S. for an extended period of months or even years. Our goal is to detect TB when such visitors, or those with whom they have contact, become ill and, in the case of TB, to check as soon as possible, whether it may be a drug-resistant case."

As was usual in this office, the phone started ringing, and Dr. Frontier had to interrupt his explanations. In addition to the many calls requesting detailed explanation of the reported lab test results, one call appeared relevant to the discussion with Jim Galen, who had left the office during the multiple previous calls 'to look around.' Dr. Frontier asked his secretary to bring Jim back to the office.

The call was from Dr. Megan Mortimer, an infectious disease specialist whom Dr. Frontier knew at the Department of Health in the neighboring state.

"Dr. Frontier, I am calling again about my patient. I would like you to know that he came from Thailand after spending almost a year serving as a member of the U.S. Peace Corp. He became ill a few months after returning to the U.S. We all know that there are outbreaks of multi-drug resistant TB (MDR-TB) in some areas of Thailand, and that is the reason I suspected that he may have drug-resistant tuberculosis. We have sent his sputum specimen not only to your laboratory, but also to one of the research laboratories in our area. They are evaluating the new rapid molecular method called GeneXpert MTB/RIF from Cepheid, Inc. Without providing a formal report, they informed us that the specimen contained tubercle bacilli resistant to rifampin, which is an indirect indication that the bacteria are most likely also resistant to isoniazid. In other words, it confirms our suspicion that our patient has MDR-TB. The problem is we don't have a formal laboratory report from the research laboratory. We also cannot exclude that the patient may have not just MDR-TB, but rather XDR-TB, extensive drug-resistant TB. That means the bacteria may be resistant not only to rifampin and isoniazid, but also to other drugs. The Cepheid procedure, if we accept the informally reported result, does not provide any information regarding susceptibility or resistance to drugs other than rifampin. Therefore, we don't know which drugs to select to treat the patient. I have heard that you have a different rapid molecular procedure to test with all other drugs. Is that true?"

"Dear Megan, as I told you yesterday, we have set up conventional procedures to isolate TB cultures from the specimen you sent us, in addition to direct drug susceptibility tests with twelve drugs. The results will be available no sooner than three weeks, if the bacteria grow as expected. As a backup, we also set up the same procedures in an automated liquid medium system. That is all we will be able to report officially, if and when the results are available.

"Now, regarding your question about the rapid molecular testing... Yes, we have evaluated a new molecular system developed by the Hain Life Science Company in Germany to perform susceptibility testing with almost all drugs. This system is already available in about thirty countries, but not yet approved by the FDA for use in the U.S. and, therefore, we cannot legally report the results obtained by this method. Tomorrow I will be able to give you a verbal report of the test results. Please consider them as informal and preliminary. The final results will follow much later based on testing by the approved conventional methods. I understand your problem and I'm sympathetic to the patient, but we don't want to lose our license, and we cannot charge you for this additional testing."

The phone conversation ended, but Jim, as expected, had several questions and comments.

"What do the terms MDR and XDR mean? Are you still going to limit the availability of this Hain test and, of special interest to me, is how much was the late Dr. Meyer involved in the introduction of this procedure?"

Dr. Frontier hesitated for a moment, but then a decision came out after a somehow prolonged pause.

"First, about the terms... MDR means 'multi-drug resistant,' reflecting resistance of the bacteria to primary anti-tuberculosis drugs rifampin and isoniazid, at least. XDR is a term for 'extensive drug-resistance,' when bacteria are resistant also to any of the three injectable drugs — kanamycin, amikacin, or capreomycin — and to one of the newest drugs called quinolones.

"Only because it may help you in your investigation and with your promise that what I am going to say will not become public knowledge, I can tell you what the reality is with using new laboratory molecular procedures to detect drug-resistance rapidly, within days rather than in weeks. The availability of such a test is of great importance in saving lives through proper and timely treatment of patients having MDR-TB and XDR-TB, thus, preventing the spread of drug-resistant tuberculosis. Formally we can only use the procedures approved by the FDA.

"Fortunately, there are loopholes in the FDA restrictions, as there are in many other government regulations. One has to know about them within the system. In our Department of Diagnostic Laboratories, we have an expert on FDA and other government regulations. His job is formally defined as overseeing implementation and observance of these regulations. He is also a valuable adviser on how to circumvent those regulations, which is needed for the sake of the patients. In regard to the Hain test, we learned that our department, because it is highly recognized by the agencies that inspect our performance, is eligible to validate and use laboratory procedures that are not approved by the FDA. We are able to do this by implementing appropriate complex experimentation, along with voluminous supporting documentation. We will start using this test next week. So far, there are only two technologists who have the knowledge and accreditation to perform the test, which inevitably has caused some friction with other people in the laboratory. Dr. Meyer was usually suspicious and even opposed to introducing new procedures he thought might jeopardize our compliance with regulations and licensing. This attitude often created negative reactions from both management and technologists."

"Another question I have, although not related to my current assignment, but rather for my general education: What about implementation of this very important rapid test beyond your laboratory, around the country, in general, particularly in the state laboratories?"

"Oh, Jim, you are placing me in a difficult situation by asking me to address a very political issue. Diagnostic laboratories in all states are part of the Departments of Health, and most of them now include TB laboratories. Operation of these laboratories is strictly regulated using only FDA approved procedures, with only few exceptions. Activities of employees in these laboratories usually are strongly regulated, including hours of work and procedures they are authorized to perform. With few exceptions, the state laboratories do not develop new procedures or implement new procedures developed elsewhere. The diagnostic procedures are provided free of charge in most states. On the other hand, private laboratories, such as in this institution, charge for the diagnostic services. However, the physicians who understand the need to perform newly developed procedures for treatment of their patients, as in the case you witnessed today, have to obtain authorization from the patient's insurance company for payment."

"Dr. Frontier, I have the impression that you are not much in favor of the regulations and of the FDA activities. Are you against regulations?"

"No…not at all. I am critical of some *excessive* FDA regulations. For example, for a pharmaceutical company to make any changes in their approved document, the FDA often requires testing that change in a multi-million dollar clinical trial, which increases the cost of the product. Sometimes, there is no need for FDA approval for many diagnostic laboratory procedures. As is typical of any government agency, the FDA is trying to elevate its importance and obtain the associated increase in federal government funding beyond the goals originally established to control the safety of various products, but in an attempt to control the activities of physicians and laboratories. Fortunately, in the U.S., activities of other organizations, such as the CDC, are limited to recommendations only, and are not mandatory. That is different from some other countries. For example, in Russia any action of a physician or laboratory is regulated by a decree by the Minister of Health. It is not realistic and it does not work. I hope the U.S. will not go in this direction. I believe that the FDA is needed, and reasonable regulations are necessary. At the same time, there are many products on the market that are not controlled at all. The largest example is the 'food supplements' and products in so-called health food markets. Moreover, some institutions outside of the pharmaceutical industry can produce medications without any supervision or control from the FDA. You remember the story in October of 2012 about an outbreak of fungal meningitis, where hundreds of people were affected and dozens died, caused by spinal (epidural) injections with a contaminated steroid solution manufactured by the compounding pharmacy in

Framingham, Massachusetts. This is an example when control and regulations are needed, but for some mysterious reason, failed to be implemented."

"Doctor, thank you for all the explanation. I am very impressed, and I can promise you that none of your secrets will be revealed, especially the facts of how you are managing to circumvent regulations and restrictions for the benefits of the patients. A question that I have pertinent to my investigation is whether the elements of your operation may create conflicts among the people, not only in your laboratory, but in the department, in general, especially the ones that may have involved Dr. Meyer?"

"Of course, some conflicts and tension are inevitable, particularly among the managerial staff, some of which is often just a power struggle among ambitious people. We do have quite a sophisticated management system created with the hope that it would boost revenue. Our top administration is considering the diagnostic laboratories as a tool for generating and increasing revenue through high-quality services related to an impeccable reputation. It was thought that a sophisticated administrative structure made it possible to generate high revenues by the diagnostic laboratories in Mayo Clinic and other institutions. In fact, such an administrative structure in those places has not been a source of revenue, but rather was created to handle the increasing revenue coming from a large number of clients from Saudi Arabia and other Arab countries. In fact, according to *The Wall Street Journal* report (April 23, 2013), there is great competition among few institutions for wealthy patients that can pay high fees for regular services. In this competition, Johns Hopkins Hospital in Baltimore opened a modern $1.1 billion building funded by the President of the United Arab Emirates and New York Mayor Bloomberg. Fundraising by Massachusetts General Hospital in Boston contributed $1.5 billion for renovation of its facilities. The Mayo Clinic is trying to attract $2 billion of private investment to upgrade the hotels in Rochester to attract wealthy patients and visitors, and even to support the substantial increase of the city population by creating jobs. On this background, we, at this institute, can compete with these financial giants by introducing new procedures that are not available there and by developing a tighter approach to a personalized medicine, not by expanding the number of administrative positions.

"Nevertheless, the administration of our diagnostic laboratories has been charged with increasing revenue, and this is one of the reasons for the tension and conflicting situations. Often, performance of the laboratory directors has been judged by the revenue growth in each laboratory. Dr. Meyer's job was to place certain pressures on each director, which often created conflict. Because Dr. Meyer was not as knowledgeable of the operation as were lab directors, he wasn't respected. The lab directors maintained that the only way to increase the revenue would be to introduce new procedures that aren't available in the state laboratories, which, as you now understand, is not an easy task.

"Another source of conflict is our interactions with John Matthew, the regulatory official whom you will meet later. John has taken advantage of his unique qualification and has assumed the role of watchdog to ensure that every technologist complies with regulations and follows the procedures protocol that was approved. He often unexpectedly appears at a technician's workbench, and writes negative comments along with various degrees of harassment. He doesn't have to do it, but this type of activity gives him a sense of power and provides him with job security. Obviously, the technicians don't like him.

"There are many other areas of internal conflict. We argue, and sometimes hate each other, but not to the degree of intending to kill. Unless..."

"Unless what, Doctor?"

"Unless there are some problems of a personal nature."

"Can you address this more specifically?"

"You know that some personal interaction is inevitable when people spend hours and days in close proximity at the bench, and even taking their lunch breaks together. Most often, it develops into simple friendship, but sometimes goes beyond that, either in a negative way or it may evolve into another type of relationship. I understand what type of interactions you are interested in, but I am not a good source for this type of information. Perhaps you or other members of your team will learn more by interviewing other people."

Chapter 5 -

Visiting the Molecular Diagnostic Lab

D r. Bharat Gupta, an elegant forty-year-old woman from India, received her Ph.D. degree in India. She was a fellow in the genetics program at University of London in England, and later attended Harvard University for further training in this field. Her participation in the Human Genome Project and as a co-author of several publications with prominent experts in molecular diagnostics, secured her position as one of the top experts of the field.

Andrew Powell came to the laboratory at nine A.M. as scheduled. "Good morning, Dr. Gupta. My name is Andrew Powell. We met at the meeting on Monday, and now I'm here, in part, to become acquainted with the operation of the department, but also because samples from Dr. Meyer's body will be submitted to this laboratory for testing."

"Yes, we are happy to have you."

"Dr. Gupta, I was told that samples from Dr. Meyer's body will be examined in your laboratory for final diagnosis. I would like to learn exactly what this testing represents. I am quite ignorant in the field of molecular biology, and would ask you to explain to me in lay language about the field of molecular diagnostics and about your operation?"

"You know the subject of molecular biology and, specifically, genetic diagnostics are quite complex areas of biology and medicine, so before I answer your questions, tell me what your level of knowledge is on this subject."

With a sly smile and feigned sarcasm, Powell said, "You mean I have to pass a test?"

Dr. Gupta smiled. "Sort of. Do you mind? It will make our discussion more clear if I know at which level I should begin to address the issues, and it will save time."

Powell's casual manner opened an avenue for candid and fruitful conversation.

"Okay, Dr. Gupta, I understand. As you probably know, basic genetics is now the topic of study in most educational programs for those who are engaged in criminal investigations. I try to stay updated in knowledge of this field as a part of the mandatory continuing education program. This is in addition to my basic education attained from high school biology classes.

"Now, here is what I can offer regarding your question. It is common knowledge that humans have forty-six chromosomes in every cell of their body. Twenty-three are inherited from the mother and twenty-three from the father. The so-called 'sex chromosomes' listed as chromosomes No. 23 are represented by two X chromosomes in females, one from the father and one from the mother. However, in males, one is a Y chromosome from the father, and the other one is an X chromosome from the mother. It is also well known that chromosomes contain *Deoxyribonucleic Acid*, commonly called DNA, which is a carrier of genetic information. Each of the two strands of this coiled structure consists of repeating arrangements of four molecules called nucleotides and known as A, G, C, and T, which stands for adenine, guanine, cytosine, and thymine. Two strands of DNA run in opposite directions, and they are connected by pairing nucleotides A + T and G + C, the connections forming the 'ring' of the stair-like double helix of DNA when arranged in various combinations, or sequences. Collections/Groups of base pairs represent genes. Each gene is numbering anywhere from a few hundred to well over a million pairs. The genes are the 'blueprints' for cells to synthesize proteins, which are ultimately responsible through a chain of reactions for most of our appearance and body functions, such as growth, development, hair color, what inherited diseases we can develop, and so on. DNA is like a software program, and our body is executing it. I've learned from my classes that according to the Human Genome Project report, there are 20,000 to 25,000 genes in the human DNA, and the variation between individuals is quite small, averaging about one percent variation in the nucleotide sequences between individuals. It is the combination of these gene differences that makes us each unique.

"The bottom line is that since 1998, criminal laboratories are now capable of detecting these differences by performing DNA profiling, referred to as 'genetic fingerprinting,' which is based on sequencing analyses of samples of blood, semen, saliva, skin, hair, etc., that might be found at a crime scene. Variations in the sequences of these combinations are strictly individual and the patterns can be traced to the suspect or to the victim. That's all I know on this subject." Powell smiled and asked, "Did I pass the test?"

"Yes and very well." Dr. Gupta smiled in return.

"I realize that my knowledge of genetics is very limited, but I am very curious about it. For example, I always heard, without understanding, about RNA along with DNA. Also, what is the mitochondrial DNA mentioned in some reports as a test for heritage? Can you explain all this?"

"Of course, Mr. Powell; the field of genetics is much broader and complex than it is presented in high school biology classes. Regarding *Ribonucleic Acid or* RNA…like DNA, it is present in every cell, and is made up of particular sequences of nucleotides. However, rather than forming two complementary strands like DNA, RNA is a single-strand chain of nucleotides, and the bases that compose this chain are slightly different from DNA. It is adenine, guanine, cytosine, and uracil instead of thymine. RNA molecules are quite fascinating in their own right, but for our purposes, you can think of them as 'go-betweens,' allowing the collection of DNA bases that form a particular gene to ultimately produce a protein. DNA is *transcribed* into this 'messenger RNA,' or mRNA, by a complex process involving many special enzymes, and then translated to yield synthesized proteins, the molecular workhorses of the cell. These processes take place in human and in any other living cell in the world.

"On the other hand, with regard to the genetics of viruses, you will hear that there are DNA- and RNA-viruses and that it is an issue when addressing the problem of using the viruses as vehicles, or so-called 'vectors' for gene therapy. I understand that all these details and terms are overwhelming, but there are more. The reason for mentioning all this is to indicate that handling the genetic work requires exceptional technical skills and expertise by trained professionals, which means that someone cannot just drop in and begin performing genetic work just by assignment."

"Another question: What is the mitochondrial DNA?"

"Okay, this is a piece of information that you can use in your future education in genetics. Along with the large DNA molecules present in the nuclei of our cells, there is another type of DNA called mitochondrial DNA, or mDNA, which is present not in the nucleus, but in the cytoplasm, in organelles called mitochondria which control the energy metabolism in the cell. Mitochondrial DNA is much smaller than the nuclear DNA, as it is coding for only thirty-seven genes, and is inherited from the mother *only* in humans and many other species. It is passed from mothers to all of their offspring. Using mDNA, some scientists believe they are able to trace human lineage back to a primordial 'Eve,' from whom the vast majority of humans appear to have descended. This feature is used to trace maternal lineage far back in time, through generations as a genealogical DNA test. Perhaps, it can be used in your professional work."

"Thank you. It is very interesting and, perhaps, can be very useful in criminology. I'm sorry for having interrupted you, but let's go back to the operation of your laboratory."

"May I ask you, before I give you an overview of our work here, what do you know about genetic diagnostics and gene therapy?"

"Not much, except that I was told it may be the path for the future of medicine, and that molecular diagnostic tests may be useful for detecting illnesses that are difficult to diagnose with common tests. In addition, as I understand, it may be useful in predicting the probability of some illnesses in an individual by finding a mutation of certain genes. You must bear in mind that it has become difficult nowadays to separate fiction from truth with the prevalence of so many sci-fi videos, movies, and even video games about using various genes to replace the malfunctioning gene and even various functions."

"That is true, and the reality of science often exceeds many of the wildest fantasies. You mentioned the word 'mutation,' and so, detection of these mutations is the basis of our genetic diagnostic work. You must realize that what we call mutations are actually changes in the DNA sequence and they occur in different ways. Some of them, hereditary mutations, can be inherited from parents and are transmitted down through generations. Other mutations can be acquired, and not passed through generations, often caused by environmental factors during the person's life through mistakes in DNA replication during the cell division.

"The human genome was sequenced in 2003, and the cost of this multi-center study, called the Human Genome Project, was about $2 billion. Since then, individual sequencing has improved and the price has decreased. The procedure is now automated through the development of instrumentation, including DNA sequencers and the cost is now approximately one thousand dollars. On this table is a sequencer, which provides results within forty-eight hours. Future development will lead to a more rapid turnaround time and lower the cost of the test. Individual sequencing of DNA is what we do in this laboratory. Detection of 'defective' genes is the purpose of testing to diagnose an illness that cannot be detected by usual laboratory methods. It is our hope that, in the near future, this information will lead to the proper therapy, including replacement of specific genes."

"Can you give me some examples of illnesses diagnosed on the basis of DNA sequencing and what is actually available now?"

"First, you must remember that beyond these discoveries on illnesses from gene mutations, single-gene diseases, there are other genetic diseases, as well, such as those caused by abnormalities of chromosomes, their number, or structure. With regard to gene abnormalities, it is important to distinguish between probability of a certain disease appearing at some time during a person's lifetime and actually detecting what is already in the body.

"One of the most important fields of development is detection of the mutated genes responsible for various types of cancer. For example, there are genes marked as BRCA1 and BRCA2, which have been identified as carriers of the mutations indicating high probability of breast and ovarian cancers."

"Dr. Gupta, sorry for interrupting you again, but I have another question. What do you do if such a mutation is detected?"

"It is interesting to note that most women prefer to not know and, therefore, don't go through the testing. Conversely, those who are tested and learn that they do have these defective genes are challenged with making a very tough decision. This issue was addressed in an article published in the May 14, 2013 edition of *The New York Times* about famous actress Angelina Jolie. Genetic testing indicated that she had a mutation in these genes, and her doctors told her that she had an eighty-seven percent risk of breast cancer and a fifty percent risk of ovarian cancer. This was in addition to a strong family history of the disease; her mother died from breast cancer. She decided to get a preventive double mastectomy, which decreased her probability of getting cancer to less than five percent. Also reported in the same article was that a twenty-four-year-old Miss America contestant, Allyn Rose, announced that she was undergoing a preventive mastectomy due to a strong family history of breast cancer, in addition to having the BRCA1 defective gene."

"Is it becoming a standard approach for women to check for mutations in these two genes?"

"Not at all. It is still a controversial issue, and the subject of discussions among the professionals. The experts suggest performing such testing for those who have a strong family history. Also, breast cancer can occur in women who don't have these mutations. One should keep in mind women who have one or two of these mutations have a sixty percent risk for breast cancer compared with twelve percent for women without such mutations."

"Sorry, again, for interrupting you. These stories are fascinating, and perhaps decisions on preventive mastectomy require a lot of bravery of the woman and support of her family. But let's continue. You were going to indicate other examples of the genetic testing benefits."

"Yes, there are many. One of them is the prediction of a high probability of lung cancer by finding a specific mutated gene. Regarding some cancers, there is a new development for sequencing the cancer cells obtained through biopsy or surgery. The results may indicate details of the type of the cancer and, subsequently, direct a more appropriate selection of anti-cancer drug, instead of the long-term practice where doctors try one drug after another until the appropriate one is found. There are coordinated studies by several research institutions, such as the 'Cancer Genome Atlas Project' funded by the National Institutes of Health, which is targeting development of the anti-cancer drugs based on specific mutations in patients' tumors, as referred to in *The Wall Street Journal* on May 2, 2013.

"The most striking recent developments were reported in the April 24, 2013 edition of *The Wall Street Journal.* The study was based on analyses of fifty-five genes and using the co-called SynapDx biomarker technology for early diagnosis of autism, and a similar VenPsych blood test for diagnosis of schizophrenia. These discoveries are the focus of public attention, as you can see from publications in *The WSJ.*"

"What about other predictions of illnesses that a person may develop in the future?"

"Well, here are some more examples. Genetic testing can be used for detection or predicting some eye problems, such as macular degeneration and other retina-related conditions. Another example of diagnostic use of DNA sequencing is in detections of certain heart conditions, such as arrhythmia, which is an irregular and/or fast heartbeat. This condition may cause collapse, stroke, or even death by a sudden cardiac arrest brought on by excessive physical activities or strong emotions. These conditions can often be, but not always, detected by EKG. This abnormality also may not be seen on autopsy and only detected by genetic testing."

"Some newspapers keep publishing stories stating that genome sequencing in healthy people may predict whether a person has an increased probability of getting cancer or another serious illness due to defective genes, and, in this way, predict an individual's fate. Is your laboratory involved in such testing?"

"It is a controversial issue and, so far, we are not performing such tests in this laboratory. Since sequencing is now becoming affordable, some people compare the cost of this test to a preventive colonoscopy, and it may become an issue as to whether or not to use it as another preventive test. This will allow a patient and his or her doctor to make an informed decision, take certain precautions, or even preventative measures. On the other hand, such information may produce damaging psychological effects. It is a controversial issue, and we don't routinely perform such tests in this laboratory. At least, not for now."

"I know the time is limited for you and for me, but can you to give me a short overview of the future perspectives of medical genetics, since it is an essential part of future activities of this institution?"

"In short, this research field is very broad, much broader than we just discussed. For example, there are several types of so-called genetic diseases. Among them are those that are related to the entire chromosome, the missing, the duplicated, etc., to a single gene disorder, and those caused by an alteration in the mitochondrial DNA."

"Dr. Gupta, we began our conversation with the term 'gene therapy.' I was going to visit the Genetic Research Laboratory to learn about this issue, but I'm told that as part of their collaboration with the industry, and because of proprietary and political reasons, it is off limits. In general terms and for my education, can you tell me what progress has been made in gene therapy, and how realistic is therapy when a defective gene is detected?"

"As you know, the function of my laboratory is limited to the diagnostics only, and I am not involved in the activities of the Genetic Research Laboratory. So, I can address only issues that are common knowledge and are available in publications, or on the Internet."

"I would appreciate any information, since I don't have time to search the literature on this subject."

"Currently, it is still in the embryonic stage of development with few successful exceptions. The idea of transporting a normal functional gene into the cell's nucleus containing a defective gene for replacement goes back to 1972. Such transport requires a delivery vehicle, 'delivery vector,' for which a modified virus or its fragment can be used. Other potential delivery vectors, instead of viruses, are liposomes and Nanoparticles. The first attempts of gene therapy were made in the 1990s in the U.S. with the FDA approval, and in Europe. These attempts resulted in complications and several deaths, and were discontinued. In 2003, the FDA placed a temporary hold on gene therapy trials.

"Only after 2006, some promising results were reported from trials in treating blindness caused by the retinal disease called amaurosis, as well as chronic myelogenous leukemia, and even Parkinson's disease. After years of intensive research, including more than fifteen hundred experimental trials, the interest in gene therapy was renewed as a potential for treating rare forms of blindness, hemophilia, and some heart conditions. In addition to these examples, there has been progress in treating progressive blindness due to age-related macular degeneration of the retina, and some success was achieved by transplantation of fetal retinal cells."

"Dr. Gupta, I read an article in the May 16, 2013 edition of *The Wall Street Journal* about the possibility of human cloning in the future, and the authors from Oregon Health and Science University suggested using the same procedure for treatment of various illnesses and injuries. What do you think about it?"

"Perhaps, the described procedure might become one of the genetic therapies in the future. The procedure consists of several steps. First, in an unfertilized human egg the DNA is replaced with the patient's skin cell containing the DNA of the patient. After they are implanted into the womb and with certain manipulation, the cells begin to develop into an embryonic cell. After removal of this artificial 'embryo' into the *in vitro* conditions, the cells can be developed into embryonic stem cells, which through certain complex manipulations can be differentiated into a desired cell type, such as heart, nerve, muscle, or bone tissues. Such artificially created tissues can be injected into the animal body — or human in the future — to replace the damaged tissue. As I have said, it is still one of the plans for the future, but it is exciting."

"Yes, as *The WSJ* article said, this was the first time it was demonstrated that it is possible to create cloned embryonic stem cells that are genetically identical to the person from whom they are derived. I feel that it is still far into the distant future, including the controversial issue of human cloning, but what is the situation today? Are any of the gene therapies available now?"

"The very first gene therapy agent ever approved by the European Union, only in 2012, for practical use, was Glybera, for treatment of a rare lipoprotein lipase deficiency (LPLD). This deficiency is caused by errors in the pattern of the gene that codes for a protein called lipoprotein lipase (LPL). Glybera introduces a normal LPL gene packaged in a delivery vector derived from adeno-associated virus (AAV). This virus has a natural propensity toward muscle cells, the tissue which normally contributes to healthy LPL protein production. As I said, if you have time, you can find more details on the Internet. Reports on promising results of gene therapy are not only appearing in scientific journals, but also in *The Wall Street Journal*, as an indication of the importance of this development. One of such sensational report appeared in the March 21, 2003 edition. It was about the successful treatment of patients with leukemia by gene manipulation of the immune system. As I have said before, gene therapy is still in its infantile stages. There are several approaches for gene therapy. One is when the patient's cells are taken from the body and reinserted after the proper genes are altered. The other option is when such genetic manipulation and replacement is done with the targeted cells in the body.

"The most recent approach is replacing and inserting normal genes using various delivery vectors, including modified viruses. For example, as recently reported in the May 30, 2013 edition of *The WSJ,* one of the inactivated adeno-associated viruses (AAV-9) is suggested by the University of Pennsylvania gene-therapy program, to be used as a vector to transport genes that stimulate the nasal cells to produce some universal antibodies against a broad range of flu and flu-like viruses. Again, so far, it is done only on mice. "

"Thank you, Dr. Gupta. May I ask you one more question? What are the major obstacles in developing gene therapy?"

"Again, as reported in the literature, there are at least three or four major problems. One of them is that most health problems are caused by the combined effect of mutations in multiple genes, while gene therapy is so far promising only for illnesses caused by mutation of a single gene. Another problem is the difficulties in providing long-term stability of the DNA after its delivery into the target cell. Finally, as delivery vectors of the DNA, some viruses may reverse from being non-virulent and become the cause of a viral infection. Other viruses may cause an immune response and rejection, and some viruses, despite modification, may still remain toxic, and even trigger a malignant transformation.

"In addition, there are some obstacles in genetic diagnostic testing. Many companies continue to offer a number of tests, including sequencing of a patient's entire genome. This situation has already caused some problems, including ethical, patient privacy, legal, and political. Another problem is licensing of the gene molecules, even if it is separated from the patient's body. To complicate matters, many insurance companies in the U.S. may begin to raise premiums for those who are found to have 'bad genes.'

"Along with progress in this field, the legal issues continue to mount and, from time to time, this issue is debated by the Supreme Court, particularly the issue of patenting genes. Development of molecular biology, genomic diagnostics, and gene therapy has a high level of commercial potential. For example, in 2010, the need for these studies generated \$120 million in global sales of stem-cell products, and is predicted to increase to \$7 billion by 2020.

"The ethical part of 'ownership' of the parts of human-origi-nated substances has an interesting history. The term 'HeLa cells' is a code name, which originated from the misinterpretation of name Helen Lane, whose real name was Henrietta Lacks, and HeLa cells were isolated from her cervical cancer, from which she died in 1951. This cell line became the most important tool in various fields of ex-perimental medicine, particularly in gene mapping, cloning, vaccine development, etc. These cells were sold and widely distributed in many countries around the world during a period of more than sixty years. Henrietta Lacks was a poor black tobacco farmer, whose fam-ily never profited from this venture and never gave consent for these events. The story of the collision between ethics, race, and medicine surrounding Henrietta Lacks was revealed only in 2010 by Rebecca Skloot in her book titled *The Immortal Life of Henrietta Lacks*, which became a popular #1 *New York Times* bestseller.

"Along with the controversies surrounding the legal problems of the growing number of genetic diagnostic tests, there is a proposal of the so-called 'Direct-to-Consumer Testing,' a method by which anyone can screen his/her own genes without authorizations and regulations. Such procedures, described in the accessible literature and on the Internet, can be used for finding the disposition of an in-dividual to various cancers, cystic fibrosis, heart disease, etc."

"Dr. Gupta, I am very grateful to you for your time and pa-tience with me. I have learned so much and hopefully this knowl-edge will be useful in my future work."

"No problem. Perhaps we will meet again when I receive Dr. Meyer's samples' test results, which may be some time next week."

Suddenly, the telephone rang. It was a reminder for Dr. Gupta that, in ten minutes, she was to head to a previously scheduled meeting in the Vice President's office. After saying goodbye to Mr. Powell, she rushed to the meeting. It was rare that she was honored to attend high-level meetings.

Chapter 6 -

Genetics for Medicine of the Future

L ife at the universities and research institutions consists of many meetings, held monthly, weekly, and daily. These meetings are held by small, large, pre-scheduled, emergency, divisional, and special groups. Most people dislike these meetings, but some feel that they are necessary. It is obvious that individuals in administrative positions place a high value on all these meetings. After all, it is a significant part of their jobs that gives them the sense of being in command and in power. Also, important decision-making in these meetings removes individual responsibilities if the wrong decisions are made. Anyway, meetings represent an important part of life of institutions like the Institute for Applied Immunology.

Judging from the list of individuals invited, it was clear that this meeting highly important. All lab directors, Jim Dellinger, and Dr. Higgins, Chairman of the Department of Medicine, came to Clinton's office.

Clinton said, "There are two major issues on the agenda today. One is the formulation of the 'Mission of the Institute,' and the second is the progress of our project on gene therapy, which is under contract with the 'Company.' For the second part, only a few of you will need to remain, but for now let's discuss our future in general terms. Dr. Higgins will address the first issue. Please, Dr. Higgins."

"There is a request from NIH and other government agencies that our Institute should have a clear statement of our mission. This statement is important for continuing financial support due to the competition for funds among the number of universities and scientific groups interested in the development and applications of the genetic research. It will be discussed in all departments, and now I would like to have input from your department, which is going to be the major part of our future development. The Board of Directors recommended that after completion of the upcoming development phase, we should consider changing our name to 'Institute of Personalized Medicine.'

This suggestion was made considering accumulation of future knowledge that would determine a patient's genetic profile, which would not only include genetic and non-genetic factors, but also environmental factors as the basis for the most effective therapy. One detail in this development is obvious. This goal can be achieved only by broadening the current DNA sequencing with involvement of a number of laboratories, at least for analyses of the test results. I would like you to submit a short, but comprehensive proposal from your department. However, for now, let's begin with preliminary discussion. Dr. Gupta, let's hear your input."

Dr. Gupta stated, "I believe that we are not talking about the document, but rather about the general plans for the future. I am very impressed with this plan, and am looking forward to it. To assess the patient's genome, determination of the patient's genetic profile by DNA sequencing will include not only analyses of current health status, but also predisposition to cancer, heart diseases, and diabetes. That is an ethical, legal, and social problem, and it will require availability of genetic counseling. I would also like to mention that the major tool for this program is the DNA sequencing, which is now automated and becoming more technically user-friendly. Of course, it can be done in a number of laboratories, but economically it may be rational to perform it in one place, and send the results to other laboratories for interpretation."

Dr. Sandoval said, "Of course, the key element of future development is research on gene therapy, particularly the issues of designing safe and effective vectors to transport the therapeutic genes. We will discuss this further during the second part of our meeting. However, I would like to mention that additional coordination of future involvement of diagnostic laboratories will need to be established, and should be built beyond the current administrative structure of the Department of Diagnostic Laboratories."

Dr. Michael Gilman, Director of the Pharmacology Laboratory, volunteered to speak next. "As you know, the efficiency and speed of individual responses to the administered drugs are quite variable, and the developing idea is that analyses of several risk factors in the person's genetic profile can predict the person's most likely positive response or serious adverse reaction to the administered drug. This approach, called pharmacogenetics, is not yet fully developed, but it is becoming a very important field of medicine, since millions of people are hospitalized because of serious adverse drug reactions, and thousands of them die from them. Such analyses may help in better selection of drugs. I think we will be able to do this type of work."

Director of the Immunology Laboratory Dr. Peter Vincent said, "One of the important research and applications in the field of immunogenetics has been on prediction and gene therapy of genetically-based autoimmune diseases such as multiple sclerosis, diabetes type I, and rheumatoid arthritis. Now, with the affordability of the DNA sequencing procedure, we will be able to address both detection of genetic dispositions that may help in diagnosis and prediction of the autoimmune diseases, as well as appropriate research which in the future, will lead to gene therapy."

Dr. David Brinkley, Director of the Core Laboratory, said, "To avoid duplication and confusion in regard to the need for results in different laboratories, we will need to create an algorithm for coordinated testing of the patients' specimens. I would suggest that the specimens be sent to the Core Laboratory, and we will make proper arrangements for testing and distribution of the results. Another issue that we should decide is whether we will participate in the population screening for genetic diseases that will eventually be requested."

Mr. Clinton stood up and said, "Thank you all for your thoughts and suggestions. I am asking Dr. Dellinger to prepare a short document with all the suggestions and present it directly to Dr. Higgins, and also to chair a committee consisting of all lab directors to coordinate future development related to the Department of Diagnostic Laboratories. Let's now adjourn this meeting, and I would ask Drs. Dellinger, Gupta, and Sandoval to remain."

Dr. Bharat Gupta was surprised and impressed that, beside herself, only Dr. Jim Dellinger and Dr. Maryann Sandoval were invited to Edward Clinton's office. Dr. Gupta knew Maryann from her days at Harvard University. Both were in training at the same time, but Bharat actually did not care for her, so much to the point of envy toward Maryann. Although Maryann had never performed routine diagnostic work, she was assigned to a more prestigious job in research. Even more surprising, was the invitation to participate in a discussion on the issue of gene therapy research conducted by Maryann, as followed from Clinton's introduction.

"To begin, I want to stress that our discussion here is strictly confidential. There will be no minutes or notes. At this time, we must address the issues that are most important to our institution. We have a contract with a company for the development of gene therapy, and it is through the funding of this company that the Genetic Research Laboratory exists. In this meeting, we will discuss the guidelines for future research, interactions with the 'Company,' and our goals beyond the existing contract. First, I will ask Dr. Sandoval to update us on our obligations with the 'Company.'"

After a short pause, Dr. Sandoval said, "Initially, the 'Company' was interested in development methods for direct delivery of therapeutic genes into the patient's body via packaged Nanoparticles. That was in line with the 'Company's' primary direction to develop various uses of Nanoparticles in medicine. After the initial phase of our collaboration, we concluded that this direction is hardly going to be efficient. Despite the seeming simplicity of this approach, it appeared that it was very difficult for the injected gene to achieve access to chromosomes in a specific organ or tissue. Therefore, we focused our emphasis on developing the indirect approach, which was to insert the therapeutic gene into the stem cells or genetically engineered viruses that are used as delivery vectors. The 'Company's' interest is to choose Nanoparticles to be introduced into genetically manipulated stem cells, a process called *transfection*, and to use these cells as a delivery vector of the therapeutic gene."

"Dr. Sandoval, before you go further, can you explain to us the basics of the Nanoparticles?"

"That is a growing trend. Nanoparticles can be thought of as delivery capsules that are very small, less than a hundred Nanometers, approximately the size of most viruses. It is possible to encapsulate various medications, such as anti-cancer drugs and antibiotics, into these particles, and when injected into the human body they create a 'depot' from which the drug is slowly released, instead of giving the patient multiple injections. In addition, Nanoparticles are used to deliver drugs to various tissues, such as the brain, that are not accessible for many drugs in solutions. Nanoparticles are supposed to consist of biodegradable materials, which supposedly make them harmless when injected into the human body. The issue of Nanoparticles being 'harmless' is often the subject of discussions among the experts.

"The history of Nanoparticles is quite interesting. They were originally developed in Germany in the 1970s, and later some Russian scientists learned of their potential usefulness not only for therapeutic purposes, but also as a vehicle for biological weapons. Nanoparticles can preserve viruses, bacteria, and toxins incorporated in them, enabling them to become stable in the environment when used as aerosols released into the air. In the former Soviet Union, they created special institutions for developing all forms of biological weapons, including those that used Nanoparticles. Today, Nanoparticles are being used around the world to develop new forms for delivery of medications."

"Thank you, Dr. Sandoval. Now let's get back to our discussion. The next question is what stem cells are used in your research?"

"There were reports on success of using both embryonic and adult stem cells. For example, there are claims that human skin cells can be converted into brain cells and then used to treat mice that have myelin disorders, a family of diseases that includes multiple sclerosis. An article appeared in *The Wall Street Journal* in 2003 entitled '*Research Offers New Hope for Multiple Sclerosis.*'

"Despite these and other sensational reports, we believe that the use of human embryonic stem cells is much more promising. They are more functional than adult stem cells for genetic manipulations such as introducing therapeutic genes and differentiation into various cell types, such as liver, pancreas, cardiac, etc. Moreover, they grow quite rapidly and remain stable *in vitro*. Nevertheless, intensive research is necessary for optimization of conditions in which the cells are cultivated to eliminate many known and unknown undesirable complications in maintaining embryonic stem cell lines. That is what we are doing now, with systematic reports to the 'Company,' as is outlined in our contract with them."

"Now, the focus of our discussion that is the most confidential, and the question is what we are not reporting to the 'Company,' what must we report, and what don't we need to report, from other experiments that you are doing and are planning to do? On this issue, I would like to have comments and opinions first from you, Dr. Sandoval, followed by Dr. Dellinger and Dr. Gupta."

"Well, as I have reported before, we began using the same embryonic stem cell line as that used for the research under the 'Company's' project, but in the way that these cells are inoculated not with the Nanoparticles containing genes, but with genetically manipulated viruses containing the genes. This process is called *transduction* in the literature. It appears to be quite promising; however, very sophisticated genetic manipulations with the viruses are required to make the virus safe, not toxic, and not tumor-stimulating. At the same time, it has to be an efficient vehicle for the inserted therapeutic gene. Some scientists believe that it is better to not rely on viruses as vectors of the genes, but, perhaps, both avenues should be pursued in research at this time."

Dr. Gupta said, "Thank you for inviting me to participate in this discussion. I believe, as much as I know about the subject from the recent literature, both directions of research using transfection and transduction is quite promising. I would recommend maintaining the contract with the 'Company' requiring use of Nanoparticles for delivery of genes into the stem cell, and, at the same time, developing a project for using the modified viruses for the same purpose. In my opinion, perhaps using viruses *instead* of Nanoparticles may become the winner in the end, but requires very intensive engineering virology work. Regarding the legal and political issues, I believe that the additional work with viruses should proceed beyond the 'Company's' existing contract, by using the institution's internal resources and in complete confidentiality. If we achieve success, patenting could become a major issue."

Dr. Dellinger felt that he should contribute to the discussion. "We do have in our institution a very skillful virologist who is also trained in genetics — Dr. Boris Filatov. He is from Russia where he was involved in viral engineering for developing various vaccines, and he has received a lot of training in the U.S. The problem with engaging Dr. Filatov is not that we can't trust him, but that we cannot pay his salary from the grant provided by the 'Company.' They would immediately realize that we are conducting research beyond the contract by using the 'Company's' resources. I would like to propose that we transfer Dr. Filatov into the Genetic Diagnostic Laboratory as part of his promotion, but under the condition that, in reality, he would do research with the viruses, if such an arrangement is acceptable by all parties involved, and remains confidential."

After a short period of silence, Mr. Clinton tried to resume the discussion, but nobody volunteered any new suggestions. Everyone was immersed in deep thought. However, it seemed that Dr. Sandoval was trying to hide her feelings. The thought that she was about to lose her monopoly on gene therapy research was deeply upsetting. What she didn't know was that Dr. Dellinger already suspected that she had made significant progress in her work with the selected viruses, and furthermore, she had kept it secret from everybody, including Dr. Dellinger, her formal boss. This was the primary reason Dr. Dellinger suggested having this meeting at Mr. Clinton's office. He thought that it would serve as an avenue for disclosure of any new findings by Dr. Sandoval. Mr. Clinton understood the situation, and was concerned about patenting if the research proved successful. Inviting Dr. Gupta to the discussion and suggesting Dr. Filatov's involvement in genetic research were among the tools they were using to prevent Dr. Sandoval from monopoly and possibly taking her secrets elsewhere.

Nevertheless, in the spirit of democracy, Mr. Clinton suggested, "I am grateful to all of you for expressing your opinions, but let us think things over, and resume our discussion next Wednesday at ten A.M., and we'll continue to have weekly meetings on this subject. Hopefully, Dr. Filatov will join us next time. In the meantime, I will discuss the situation with the president to make final decisions for the future. I agree that Dr. Filatov should be involved in the research with viruses, but, perhaps, it would be wise to keep his involvement undisclosed. I will discuss with Dr. Crowley the possibility that Dr. Filatov will keep his office in the Microbiology Laboratory and, perhaps, they will have some space there for his experiments. In addition, he will need one or two technicians. I will also discuss with the President, the possibility of getting financial support for this additional research from one of the board members."

With that, Mr. Clinton adjourned the meeting and said, "Thank you, again, and see you all next week."

Chapter 7 -

Cause of Death Identified

The meeting on Wednesday convened as scheduled at ten A.M. in the Vice President's office, but the agenda was suddenly changed due to new information regarding the cause of Dr. Meyer's death. The attendees of this meeting were Mr. Powell from the FBI, Chairman of the Department of Medicine Dr. Charles Higgins, Dr. Dellinger, and Dr. Gupta.

Mr. Clinton said, "I believe that the problem regarding Dr. Meyer's death is resolved. First of all, the CDC reported that there were no pathogens, either bacteria or viruses, detected in his body, nor any poisons. In addition, it was reported that the man from India, whose tissue samples Dr. Meyer was involved in testing, died from a generalized staph infection that originated from a wound on his foot. Samples from Meyer's body were delivered Monday to our Molecular Diagnostic Laboratory. Dr. Gupta expedited DNA sequencing, and today we have the results. Please, Dr. Gupta."

"We performed complete genome sequencing, and found three mutated defective genes responsible for controlling the flow of potassium ions between the cells in the heart muscle. Mutations in these genes, marked as KCNH2, KCNJ2, and KCNQ1, increase the

---

activity of the protein channels transporting the potassium ions. As a result, disruption in ion transport alters the way the heart beats, leading to abnormal heart rhythm. This abnormality is the basis of a genetic heart disease, which was formally recognized only in the year 2000 and called 'short QT syndrome', or SQTS, although some physicians had diagnosed this disease in their patients long before. It may be a cause of death in young and not very young, athletes, with a frequency of one per 100,000. The name of this syndrome originated from the QT interval on the EKG when it is shorter than the normal 300 milliseconds. This syndrome is detectable on EKG, but often overlooked. Dr. Meyer never had an EKG; he considered himself very healthy. Given the fact that he died after the extensive physical activity of playing hockey, is typical of SQTS."

"Dr. Higgins, what is your opinion?"

"I believe that we have enough data showing the cause of Meyer's death. That is in addition to the work done at the CDC. An increase in the number of deaths from SQTS has been reported in literature in the last few years as physicians are becoming more aware of it. In some countries, EKG testing among athletes is becoming mandatory. I think that we should appreciate the work done in Dr. Gupta's laboratory, for the expedited testing and clear results."

Mr. Powell stood up and after looking around expecting some attention said, "I would first like to thank everyone for your collaboration and productive interaction with me and my two agents. Meetings with your colleagues have been a challenge for us, and we have learned a lot. Also, I should note it is not surprising that there were no sinister activities among the employees of this department related to Dr. Meyer's death. Our investigation here is finished, and we are closing the case. We will forward our conclusion to the Police Department, as well. I would like to ask that the detailed medical report, with all the test results and description of the final diagnosis as to the cause of death, be submitted to us."

In fact, Mr. Powell withheld his suspicion that some of the employees might be involved in Meyer's death. Powell had worn the cloak of suspicion ever since he could remember; professionally it had served him well, but in his personal life, its crushing weight proved to be more than most could or would bear. In this particular case, Rebecca Brown was the object of Powell's propensity toward suspicion. Two salient factors stood out — one was her past relationship with Meyer and subsequent jealousy; another was her access to pathogenic bacteria and viruses that could be used to kill Dr. Meyer. However, for now, he would keep his reasons to himself.

News of Mr. Powell's summation was forwarded to the employees of the department, causing a collective sigh of relief, particularly among those who felt they were being carefully scrutinized. Dr. Meyer died of natural causes; there was no indication that he was poisoned, nor were bacteria or viruses from the department stock used to end Dr. Meyer's life. Nevertheless, this dramatic episode caused some people to rethink their lives. Derrick's death and the subsequent investigation had a profound effect on Gloria West, and she began looking for a job elsewhere. Rebecca Brown also missed Dr. Meyer, although her relationship with him ended long before his death. She missed, while he was around, the opportunity of negative feelings toward him, bordering on hate. By her nature, she needed a target of hate and, subconsciously, looked for any misdeed committed by an unsuspecting co-worker.

Rebecca felt emptiness in her heart. Even attending her favorite games or watching them on TV did not bring any relief. She started focusing on her job, and intensified her supervisory activities, enjoying the power she had over the technicians. Every day she surveyed the laboratory, pointing out petty deficiencies — someone did not perform a test before noon, but postponed it until afternoon; someone did not replace the mask, as required; someone did not maintain sufficient records of a procedure they had performed; and someone did not perform a quality control test exactly as required in the manual, etc. Such were opportunities for Rebecca to reprimand a technician, often in a rude manner. Rebecca took perverse pleasure in writing up any of her subordinates' deficiencies and reporting them to the Human Resources Department to be entered into the person's file as a threat for potential termination. Flaunting the power of her position in this way fed her self-aggrandizement, but other, more highly placed individuals weren't immune to her cunning and deceit. No, Rebecca had bigger fish to fry, starting with Dr. Crowley, and working her way through Human Resources, the Department of Medicine, or the Department of Finance.

So great was her obsession with power and recognition that she felt impervious to criticism or reprimand. Only a few people who were sufficiently submissive to Rebecca avoided this harassment, but others soon began to complain about her behavior. As a result, Dr. Dellinger strongly reprimanded her. He also brought up some other problems related of her performance, particularly those regarding the tone of her conversations with clients calling for the results of testing. Rebecca was stunned when the Executive Director reprimanded her for overstepping her boundaries. She realized that in the substance and the delivery of this conversation, there was a real threat of being fired. Although, in the past, she enjoyed participation in the procedure of firing others as an indication of her power, the possibility of such an event happening to her was horrifying.

The usual protocol included an unannounced visit by the immediate supervisors and the head of the Human Resources Department, suggesting that he or she collect their personal belongings, and then accompanying them to the exit door.

Imagining such a humiliating occasion created in her paranoid mind, nightmares and horrifying awakenings during the night. Her nightly fantasies were filled with scenarios of murdering Jim Dellinger, but in real life she decided that she would rather die than be fired. Although she changed her supervisory style and tried to improve her relationship with the laboratory employees, the nightmares continued to dominate her mind, and Jim Dellinger became a predominant target of her hatred. Rebecca found a gun that had been stowed away and slowly removed the silencer. She started carrying it concealed in her underwear. She would kill Dellinger, and then herself, if he came with others to escort her out of the lab. It was uncomfortable, but gave her a wary sense of confidence. Once, the inevitable happened. Rebecca's husband Mark found the gun, and Rebecca confessed that she feared Dellinger would fire her. Mark took Rebecca's words seriously, and calmed Rebecca down. He assured her that he would take care of Dellinger if anything happened. This episode significantly improved their relationship. She stopped carrying the gun, but was still tormented by her fear. Unfortunately, she never again tried to talk with Dr. Dellinger, who in fact, did not care about Rebecca anymore.

Jim Dellinger's mind was preoccupied with completely different problems. His divorce was not moving forward, due to unresolved real estate problems and other financial arrangements. His interactions with Martha started cooling off, and very likely they would not marry. Problems from the past began to haunt him in a form of claims by three women from New Jersey. These women were seeking large sums of money. Quitting his job in New Jersey and moving to Montana did not put to rest his philandering past, and now his reputation was in danger! With this background, new problems began to emerge. Jim Dellinger found himself attracted to Maryann Sandoval, Director of the Genetic Research Laboratory. As often happened in the past, Jim could not keep his emotions in check when it came to interacting with a beautiful sexy woman. He became attracted to Maryann when an opportunity presented itself for his involvement in development of gene therapy; this was a promising avenue in many respects, not the least of which was financial.

Dr. Dellinger had some training in immunology while working on his Ph.D., but he was not quite as educated in molecular biology and genetics. Now he was motivated exclusively by the new opportunities this field offered, including lucrative patents that could reap a fortune in the future. He knew that his scientific imagination was quite limited, and throughout his career, he realized that a managerial position provided many advantages over being a bench-type scientist, including money, power, and controlling the activities of those doing the actual research. Moreover, some scientists that were under his administrative supervision often included his name in their publications (a well-known and silently acceptable type of bribery), which enhanced his curriculum vitae, making it appear

quite impressive. Now, at fifty-four, he had enough experience to rec-
ognize promising new trends in science. His title, the funds he controlled, and a reputation as a successful research manager usually
impressed the scientists with whom Jim offered to collaborate. With
Maryann Sandoval it was different. She was resistant to his attempts
to get involved in her research, and she was immune to his charm.

Dr. Maryann Sandoval was a statuesque woman with blonde
hair, dark blue eyes, and tan skin. She appeared much younger than
forty-six. Maryann was an experienced molecular biologist. Along
with her husband, Sam Sandoval, she received a broad range of
training at Stanford and Harvard Universities, as well as at some
pharmaceutical companies. They worked together at the Gentec
Corporation on stem cells and other means of so-called delivery vectors for gene transportation into the body. Their work with embryonic stem cells was quite successful and the results had been widely
published. They were less fortunate, as many other scientists were,
with viruses as delivery vectors.

After a few years together, she realized that she could hardly tolerate him on an intimate level. She developed, subconsciously, negative feelings toward any man. Maryann and Sam separated
without intending to divorce, and remained friends, even meeting
sometimes to discuss scientific matters. Sam, an experienced virologist, continued his work at the Gentec Corporation, and achieved
substantial progress in genetic engineering of some viruses from the
group of retroviruses. This large group of viruses includes those that
caused various tumors in animals, HIV, and other illnesses. Although some modified viruses of this group had been developed
with tropism to various target cells as vectors in gene therapy, Sam
and Maryann made a preference of developing a 'double vector,' a
process where the virus carrying a therapeutic gene is inserted into
the embryonic stem cell modified to have an affinity to the specific
tissue/organ. Along with their work with stem cells that was successful and reported, Sam also supplied Maryann with a virus strain
he developed that appeared to be a safe option. In her experiments,
she confirmed that it worked as intended, including evidence of

being safe by not showing any replication in animal experiments. They agreed not to immediately report these results and wait for a better time, taking into account the great potential of this finding, as well as the political situation, particularly because of Dr. Dellinger's elevated interest in this research, fearing he would steal such an important achievement.

Dr. Dellinger began visiting Maryann's laboratory quite frequently; inquiring about the progress of her research, but, so far, Maryann was not forthcoming. He did suspect that she was not reporting everything, especially with regard to the viral experiments. That was why he brought the issue up in high-level meetings, and engaged Dr. Boris Filatov in this research. Dellinger didn't know that Maryann wasn't divorced and that she continued to meet with Sam regarding her research. He began making passes at her. His 'special technique' used to be successful with other women in the past, but did not work this time and, eventually, unintentionally, and contrary to his plan, he became genuinely attracted to Maryann.

Intending to make another effort, Dellinger invited Maryann to his office under the pretense that a progress report to the company sponsoring the research was needed. As usual, he came to work dressed in a high-quality suit, white shirt, and impressive tie. He knew that this formal appearance usually impressed women and emphasized his high rank of importance. This fact, along with coffee and compliments about Maryann's work and her appearance, did not impress Maryann, who was not interested in this man and was annoyed by his attention.

"Dr. Sandoval, any progress in your research with the viruses?"

"Nothing new since our last meeting, but perhaps you should address this question to Dr. Filatov, whom you have appointed to work on this project. I delivered to him three viral strains with which we're working, but, perhaps, it is too early to ask, since he just started organizing his place in the Microbiology Laboratory."

Dr. Filatov started his experiments and soon realized that the three viral strains he received from Dr. Sandoval did not appear to be modified from the original source. Combined with information he obtained from a technician who was transferred from the Genetic Laboratory, Boris became suspicious that something was wrong. His suspicion was more enhanced by the interest Dr. Dellinger expressed in a conversation with Boris, by suggesting that Boris report to him directly on the progress of experiments. Some of the laboratory technicians watching Dellinger and Filatov working together referred to them as 'twins' because of the striking similarity in their physical appearances, although there was extreme difference in their faces and personalities. Despite their appearance, their interactions were not 'brotherly'.

Dr. Dellinger shared with Boris this suspicion that Dr. Sandoval was, perhaps, concealing the achieved results with the intention of patenting a new gene vector after leaving employment at this institution. With promises of future benefits and the appeal of this institution's 'patriotic' sentiments, Dr. Dellinger suggested that Boris 'investigate' the problem, including the search for hidden strains in Sandoval's laboratory while she was away on vacation. This situation was very similar to Boris's recollections of Russia, particularly from the stories his father told him about his experience in the former Soviet Union. Boris firmly rejected the offer, and informed Dellinger that he had the skills and knowledge to develop the needed viral strains. He also knew, without sharing with Dellinger, that if Dr. Sandoval were to develop the 'perfect viral strains,' she would hide them outside the laboratory in the form of a lyophilized culture, a process where tissue containing the virus is dried from a frozen state, thus, preserving it indefinitely. He surprisingly realized that Dellinger was not aware of this common procedure in microbiology. Well, was Dr. Dellinger not the expert he presented himself to be? He learned that it was better to keep such thoughts to himself.

Chapter 8 -

Stories He Told

Very bright cool days were typical for the latter part of September in Montana. People traveled around to see the changing colors of the trees. Boris enjoyed the beauty of nature by hiking on the weekends in the mountains with groups from the local mountain club. Another pleasant activity was the concerts by the symphony orchestra, often attended by visiting famous conductors and soloists. Boris was looking forward to the next concert on Friday featuring *Brahms' Symphony No.1*, conducted by Olari Elts, the famous conductor from the Baltics who was becoming very popular in Europe. In addition to Friday's concert, he was looking forward to seeing Clare. Her call to thank him for the book on Tchaikovsky renewed his anticipation of the weekend.

Three weeks earlier at another concert, Boris asked her for advice in regard to his recent interaction with Dr. Jim Dellinger. The mystery of Dr. Meyer's death had already been resolved. Since Clare had resigned from the FBI, she felt free to discuss the problem with Boris, and suggested that he inform her of any new development with this issue. Moreover, she said that she would ask one of her close friends living in North Brunswick, New Jersey, to check into Dr. Dellinger's background.

As expected, the concert was excellent. It became the new tradition by both to read before the concert about the upcoming program. Now they had learned about the many years that Brahms spent in creating this symphony in a continuing feeling of competition with Beethoven's fame. Some critics even labeled *Brahms Symphony #1* as 'Beethoven's tenth,' because of some similarities in themes and orchestration. Under the energetic direction by Olari Elts, the performance of the Brahms' symphony sounded no less powerful than if it were Beethoven. As they had done previously, Boris and Clare went for dinner after the concert.

"Boris, I have great news. I have been accepted back into the university! You have in front of you, not an FBI agent, but a free person, a student who signed up to major in history. That is the reason I am very interested in your stories. I hope my curiosity doesn't annoy you?"

"Not at all, Clare. It is a pleasure to tell my stories to people who have serious interest in them, and congratulations on becoming a student again. May I ask you, how did you develop an interest in history, and why did you interrupt your studies in the first place?"

"Briefly, here is my story. I grew up in Hartford, Connecticut, and our house was located next to the Mark Twain and Harriet Beecher Stowe Estates Museum. I used to go there when I was a child, and that's what inspired my interest in history. I would highly recommend visiting there when you get a chance. What do you know about these writers?"

"A lot, both writers were very popular in Russia, with all their books translated and published in Russian. It is interesting that *Uncle Tom's Cabin* was mandatory reading in high schools and was used as propaganda material to illustrate racism in America, even though the book was published in 1852. I learned that black people here in America have a negative perception about this book. The reason, I was told, is because the writer, although she was very sympathetic to the suffering of black people (she was even an abolitionist), appealed for better treatment of them as long as they 'knew their place.'"

"I read a lot during my high school years about American and world history, and enjoyed the first two years at the university. The reason I dropped out was financial. My mother is a nurse. My father was killed in Afghanistan, but his body was not discovered for some time and he was listed as MIA. Confirmation that he was killed in action only recently came to light and, along with it a financial arrangement, which allowed me to renew my education at the university. I hope to become a high school history teacher and contribute to enhancing the knowledge of young people in this field, which, I believe, is quite neglected."

"Thank you, Clare, and I'm sorry this brought back sad memories about your father. How was the book about Tchaikovsky?"

"Thank you. I finished reading the book. It is a fascinating story, indeed, and the author was a great historian, spending a lot of time digging up historic facts about Tchaikovsky's death. Now I am reading another book *Atlas Shrugged* by Ayn Rand. It was first published in 1957, but has again become very popular. Do you know about this book and its author?"

"I've heard about the book and about Ayn Rand, who came from Russia sometime in the 1920s. I understand, based on her short experience in the Soviet Union, she was predicting the future of America if the government took control of private enterprises."

"That is true, but you have to read the book. It is large — eleven hundred pages — but very interesting. As an example, her unconventional views impressed me in one particular paragraph. As you know, in popular literature and in movies the story of Robin Hood is a hero who took from the rich and gave to the poor. Ayn Rand posed a question about Robin Hood: Was he really a positive hero? The author's answer is no. He took from the 'wealthy,' actually from those who managed to build their wealth, and gave it to the 'poor,' who had done nothing to develop any wealth. As you know, there are politicians who try to play Robin Hood today with talks about redistribution of wealth. I don't have to tell you what happened with redistribution in the Soviet Union, you know about it very well. Ayn Rand describes how redistribution would look in the U.S. and there are many more interesting points in her book."

"Clare, I promised to tell you the story of my family. Are you still interested?"

"Yes, of course, and all this time I have been anticipating your story, especially now that I'm a history student."

"Okay. My story is in part my family's history and in part Russia's history. You've obviously noticed, Clare, my blue eyes and dark hair. Throughout my life, it has brought attention to me, but it is part of my story. My grandfather, Peter Smirnov, was born into a family with several generations of physicians and scientists, and traditionally they were very nationalistic. My grandfather, to the disappointment of his father, became a military man, not a doctor. Another disappointment to Peter's father was his marriage to a Jewish woman. His attitude softened when he became a grandfather to a beautiful boy, who had the same blue eyes as all the males in the Smirnov family. The boy also inherited black hair from his Jewish mother.

"After graduation from the military academy, just before the war with Germany, Major Smirnov was appointed as battalion commander at the western border of Russia. His battalion was among the first army groups to face the overwhelming German army on June 22, 1941. Soon, the battalion was separated from other detachments and was overrun by the Germans. Wounded survivors, including Peter, were captured as prisoners of war, and at the end of the war, were liberated from the camps by the British troops."

"Boris, how do you know all these facts?"

"My father, a famous scientist, achieved a very high level of recognition by the authorities as a molecular biologist and was allowed access to the KGB archives. He was eager to find out about his roots, but his interest was much broader, and that is how he learned his family history. It was common knowledge that at the end of the WWII, under the agreement between the allies, the liberated prisoners of war from Germany camps were handed over by the British to the Russians.

"Under Stalin's order, surrender to the enemy was treason, and this was not a secret to the British Government. Despite that, the British authorities sent thousands, including Smirnov, to Russia where they landed in Russian concentration camps, and died there shortly after they arrived. Smirnov's parents died during the war, labeled as a traitor's family. His wife re-settled in a small town in Siberia. His children's names were changed and they were placed in special orphanages.

"One of the orphans was my father, Dmitry. His archived KGB file stated that he had been adopted from an orphanage in the city of Tumen in Siberia. Around age six, in 1945 he was found in an abandoned house in a small city near Minsk, which had been liberated by the Russian troops. He was then put in the orphanage. According to KGB records, no documents were found, and the child was in severe shock. He did not speak, did not know his name, or who his parents were. The physician at the orphanage, Ivan Filatov, adopted the boy and gave him the name Dmitry. Throughout his years in Tumen, and later at Moscow University, Dmitry referred to Ivan and his wife Maria as his natural parents. Somehow, instinctively he felt that it was safer to not share his unclear sweet memories of a woman other than Maria, who he felt was his real mother. At the age of seventeen, he was tall and handsome, and the unusual combination of blue eyes and black hair made him quite attractive, popular with the girls in school, and later at the university. After graduation from the university in 1966, Dmitry married Lydia, one of his classmates. Three years later, Filatov received his Ph.D. in biology and eventually became one of Russia's leading experts in molecular biology and genetics. He traced his biological origin to the Smirnov family, using new genetic methods and one of the markers, his unusual eye-color, but most importantly his ability as a high-ranking scientist, to access old files and secret KGB archives.

"I was born in 1973, when the country began moving toward more freedom and Western orientation. Often in Russia, as is elsewhere, parents in a high position enable their children in their education and career. My parents enrolled me in a special school that taught a number of subjects in English, and later supported my progress at the university and in the graduate school of becoming an expert in molecular biology, virology, and genetics. I was married for a while, but my wife had very negative feelings about America, rejecting the idea of moving here, so we divorced. In short, that is the story of my life back in Russia."

"Thank you, Boris. I hope we can get together again to discuss some history beyond personal stories. Would you help me after I start my history classes at the university?"

"Yes, of course. What are you doing on Sunday? Would you be interested in going to the mountains for hiking?"

"That would be great. We can climb one of the peaks, either Granite Peak, the highest peak in Montana reaching 12,799 feet, or the Sacagawea Peak, which is not as high, only 9665 feet, but is closer to our place. It is in the Bridger Range."

"I would prefer something closer. Let's consult at the Mountain Club, and maybe join one of the hiking groups that usually meet at seven-thirty A.M. near the Holiday Inn hotel downtown to carpool. By the way, at that time I will have some information on Dr. Dellinger. My friend in New Jersey promised to call me tomorrow. I know you're eager to learn about it. We will talk about it on the hike."

It was a very pleasant hike. It was not cold, yet, and the ten-mile hike was not difficult. During the hike, twelve people of the group were together all the time, which prevented Clare and Boris from talking. An opportunity came after the hike while they were having lunch at the Holiday Inn restaurant.

"Boris, I want to ask you one question that has bothered me for some time. It's a question related to your knowledge about genetics. What do you think about the so-called genetically modified (GM) food products that have been widely discussed by the media?"

"In my opinion, most of the excitement on this issue is the result of the ignorance of many people, and that is a rather political issue. Some people are adamant about having everything 'natural' and object to anything 'modified' without realizing that none of our nutritious products are from 'original wild plants.' They have been modified for centuries by different means of selection. Today, such modifications are done faster by using modern genetic tools. Some religious fanatics views are against it, they say, 'Don't play God.'

"Here is an example mentioned in the literature about damage brought to the world by the environmentalists. In many developing countries, rice is the main if not the only food source, but the 'original' rice contains a very small amount of vitamin A. According to the World Health Organization, every year 250,000 to 500,000 children in these countries become blind, and half of them die because of vitamin A deficiency. A new type of rice called 'golden rice' was genetically developed, and it has a high vitamin A contents. It's been proven harmless, but because of the objections by the 'environmentalists,' it took twelve years of struggle before it was introduced in the Philippines. During this time, an estimated eight million children worldwide died because of vitamin A deficiency in their diet by not providing them with the gold rice.

"There are many other examples of such tragedies, not to mention the well-known debates about the Keystone pipeline for delivering oil from Canada through Nebraska to the Gulf, which would reduce by about forty percent America's dependence on foreign oil, and it would create many jobs. Environmentalists object to this pipeline, and they have a lot of political power in the form of votes. The famous journalist Dennis Prager has analyzed this situation, and concluded one of his articles with the following words: 'The employment of thousands of Americans, the well-being of the American economy, and American national security — all of these concerns are secondary to the environmentalist movement's view of nature *über alles.*'"

"I did anticipate your opinion on the subject of genetically modified products, but I wanted to be sure. Thanks, Boris. Now, I know that you're impatiently waiting to learn about Dr. Dellinger, but let's eat first."

"Now, can we talk about it?"

"Well, I have some information about his background in New Jersey, and that your suspicion was reasonable. He's not who he pretends to be. He was known as a womanizer at his previous job. That was the actual reason his wife kicked him out. And, at least once, he was accused of sexual harassment. Somehow, he managed to settle the problems and moved from New Jersey. He spent a lot of money to settle conflicts with those women. Some women are still after him, demanding more money to remain silent. One claimed that he forced her to have an abortion when she became pregnant by him. Yet, another woman threatened to tell her jealous husband, who had once said that he would kill him if he discovered that Jim was actually involved with his wife. That's what I have learned so far."

"Thank you, Clare. It is helpful to know about the person with whom I'm dealing. He obviously is trying to get secret information of my work with Dr. Sandoval, particularly about the viruses that may potentially become vectors in gene therapy. Perhaps, Dr. Sandoval already has such viruses from her previous research with her ex-husband, but keeps it secret. I will have to develop a strategy for revealing the secrets if I am successful."

After this discussion, Boris felt that he was armed, although without knowing whether he would ever use the new information about Dellinger. It was a pleasure to realize that he had a friend in this new country where he quite often felt lonely.

A feeling of satisfaction with the evening was way beyond just the information Boris received about Dellinger. It was the whole conversation with Clare about various subjects. It was a pleasure to meet someone with whom he could share his views and find common interests in music, books, and life, in general. Nevertheless, Boris recognized, reluctantly, that it was more than that. He was attracted to Clare's conversational style, the softness of her voice, and her very feminine appearance; she had large brown eyes and was tall and curvaceous, but there were inexplicable feminine features that captured a man's attention.

Chapter 9 -

Genetics for Biological Weapons

Having a trusted friend was great, particularly with the increasing feeling that it could develop into something more than just friendship. Nevertheless, having learned from his past experiences, Boris was always cautious in sharing anything with anybody. One such experience was the pain that gripped him because of the news he recently received from Russia. His father died from a heart attack, and Boris did not go back for his funeral. The last thing his father said to him before he left Moscow was that he should try to settle in the U.S. permanently and not ever, under any circumstances, come back, not even for his funeral. His father told him that his life might be at stake if he revealed his skills in the area of viral genetic manipulations.

As was now customary, the conversation with Clare took place over dinner after they had taken in a movie. Boris said, "Clare, I would like to discuss a very important personal problem with you, which is related to my work and potentially relevant to my safety. Since you were engaged in a criminal investigation at my institution, is it okay to discuss such matters with you?"

"First of all," she said, "the investigation into Dr. Meyer's death is over. Therefore, I am not engaged in anything at this institution.

Secondly, as friends, we can discuss any problem, even on a personal level. Tell me, what is it, Boris?"

"You see, following very serious advice from my father, when I arrived in the U.S. and until now, I have not disclosed my knowledge and skills in the field of genetic manipulations of viruses. My father died in Moscow, and I did not go to his funeral. Again, this was in accordance with the instructions he gave me when I left Russia. Puzzled? Here is another 'Russian story.'"

"Boris, maybe it is very personal and you should reconsider before telling me?"

"Yes, it is personal, but more than that, and I am very certain about telling you. The problem is that genetic engineering of the viruses can be used not only for development of vaccines and in the area of gene therapy, but also for development of biological weapons. The existence of biological warfare programs back in Russia was the reason my father tried to shield me from involvement; thus, he only informally provided me with knowledge in this field. He himself never got involved in these programs either. It is for my safety that he did not want me to come back under any circumstances, to prevent me from this dangerous engagement if Russian authorities learned about my knowledge. Now, since my dream of research came true at my current employment, I am really working on the genetic engineering of the viruses, and particularly the area of viral recombination, where in times past the Russian scientists failed. My work is not a secret, and I am preparing a paper for publication, which will reveal all the methodology in this field, and there are will no longer be any secrets! That also is according to my father's plan for my security."

"As I understand, the Russians might be concerned that you will reveal this technology here in the U.S., and they would lose the opportunity to be the only site in possession of it, e.g., of the important military advantage. Yes, I see how serious it is? What are you going to do for your safety?"

"As I said, the best defense I can think of is publication. I hope nothing happens before then."

"Boris, I am intrigued with the whole issue of the biological warfare. How serious it is? Please, can you tell me more?"

"Yes, of course. Historically, using infection as a weapon goes back to ancient times and to the Middle Ages where they used such primitive methods as throwing a dead body into the enemy's camp and, sometimes, things that were even more primitive. Nowadays, with the sophistication of laboratory technology and the ability to manufacture large masses of bacteria or viruses, it has become a real issue. During World War II, there were attempts to use biological weapons made in Japan and Russia, and after WWII, a sophisticated program of biological warfare was developed in several countries, including the former Soviet Union and the U.S. The main focus was on infections such as anthrax, plague, tularemia, smallpox, botulism, and viral hemorrhagic fever. Some experts are skeptical of the possibility of effective delivery of any of these agents to large population groups. These experts also believe that there is a small likelihood of biological attack because of such limitations as poor stability of the biological agents in the environment and low spread of infection in the infected population."

"Okay, that is history, but in our time, I remember that in 1979 there were reports of an outbreak of anthrax in Siberia, and the media was filled with speculations about whether this outbreak was of natural origin from infected meat or the result of an accident in a secret military institution manufacturing anthrax as a bioweapon. You probably know the details?"

"The whole history of the biological weapons in Russia is fascinating and most of it came to light in 1992, when one of the high-ranking leaders of the Soviet biological warfare program, Ken Alibek, defected to the U.S. Indications for such a program appeared even before publication of his sensational book *Biohazard* published by Delta in 1999. An outbreak of anthrax in 1979 in the city of Sverdlovsk, which is now Yekaterinburg, in the Ural Mountains, was the site of these episodes. The Bolsheviks murdered Tsar Nicolas II and his family in 1918 in this city.

"On April 2, 1979, once again, this place drew the attention of the world. A cloud of aerosolized anthrax bacilli appeared in the air at the outskirts of the city after a mysterious explosion in an underground tunnel connected with the so-called 'Town No. 19.' Town No. 19 was the code for the super-secret facility built deep underground in 1946 for the purpose of developing and producing biological weapons. The only connection of this facility with the outside world was through an underground railroad, leading to another military installation called 'Town No. 32.' There was a rumor that an explosion blew up this tunnel when a barrel filled with anthrax spores suddenly burst open during a shipment to storage or a testing facility. Another rumor, perhaps more reliable, was that the bacterial aerosol escaped from a newly built and improperly installed drying system in Town No. 19. During a shift-change, one of the technicians culturing anthrax in huge tanks forgot to replace a clogged bacterial filter.

"For many years, Soviet authorities covered up this episode and presented the situation of a substantial number of anthrax cases as a natural anthrax epidemic; thus, creating a complex scheme of deception. It was not until 1992 that, only in part, they acknowledged that there had been an accident. That was when Yeltsin told the American president, 'You know, Mr. Bush, we are still cheating on you. We promised to eliminate the biological warfare, and although some experts did all that was possible for me not to learn the truth, but I got them…..' To comply with the International Convention signed by the Soviet Union in 1972, Yeltsin issued on April 11, 1992 the Presidential Decree, under No. 390, that banned the development, production, or storage of biological and chemical weapons. Also, in an interview with the newspaper *Komsomolskaya Pravda* of May 27 of 1993, Yeltsin again admitted that the cause of the epidemic was military development. However, the truth of the matter remains a secret within Russia. For example, the Russian authorities admit that, as a result of the accident in Sverdlovsk, sixty-four individuals died from anthrax, but some experts in the field insist that the actual number of carefully concealed deaths was ten to twenty times greater.

"The episode involving anthrax in the Sverdlovsk (Yekaterinburg) area provided the first evidence of the broad multi-institutional system in the Soviet Union with thousands of employees preparing biological warfare agents. It must be noted that, initially, these efforts were under two Chief Directorates of the Ministry of Defense, No. 7 and No. 15, but later many more operational systems were established, in particular the *'Biopreparat'*, a civilian network of research and production employing about 35,000 people in forty-seven sites in the country.

Although the names and administrative structures changed, the same groups of people moved from one place to another to work toward the same goals. A number of these institutions, such as Vector near Novosibirsk, and Obolensk and Zagorsk near Moscow, are in operation now working on biodefense research, and most of them are open to foreign visitors. Funding for many of them comes from U.S. grants."

"Are there U.S. programs to prevent Russians from renewing their biological warfare programs?"

"Yes, there are. The International Science and Technology Center (ISTC) was established in Moscow to coordinate implementation of the U.S. grants to the Biotechnology Engagement Program (BTEP) and to the U.S. Civilian Research and Development Foundation (CRDF). The purpose of these and other programs was to develop collaboration between the U.S. researchers and former military-oriented scientists, often called 'weapon scientists,' in Russia and other former Soviet Republics to encourage them to use their skills in productive civilian science. The Bush administration funded a program, under the title 'BioShed,' providing $5.6 billion and engagement of three hundred U.S. institutions and 16,500 individuals to protect the U.S. from biological, radiological, and nuclear attacks. The effectiveness of this and other similar programs is debated in scientific and administrative groups. Some have suggested that BioShed will not protect us from genetically engineered pathogens. For example, a report from the Institute of Medicine and Research Council of the National Academies as quoted by Mark Williams in the *MIT Technology Review*, March-April 2006, stated that, '…in the future, genetic engineering and other technologies may lead to the development of pathogenic organisms with unique, unpredictable characteristics.'"

"Is there a real possibility of creating new biological weapons, and what is the current trend?"

"The *Biopreparat* system was established in Russia for enhancement of classical agents of biological warfare, and in 1980 they started a program for creating new pathogens that could be used as enhanced bioweapons. This was after the Russians signed the International Biological and Toxin Weapons Convention in 1972, prohibiting the use of biological and chemical agents, as well as development of means and devices for delivery of such agents. The majority of the scientific community remains skeptical regarding the probability of biological attacks, which is often motivated by the competition for grants, not to mention the fact that the nature of humans tend to deny such a horrible possibility."

"Boris, you know the real situation of today. What is your opinion on the possibility and potential danger of the development and application of the advanced biological weapons?"

"The unpleasant reality of today is that doubts about the possibility of the biological attacks were overruled with the emergence of the Ebola virus. Since 1976, six outbreaks of this deadly infection — five in Africa and one in Marburg, Germany — occurred naturally, due to infection from monkeys. Ebola, which is similar to smallpox, but much more severe with rapid progression of the lethal hemorrhagic fever, is classified by the CDC as a Class A biological terror agent. This means that this virus has the particular ability for rapid transmission and highly negative effects on public health. Failure to develop a vaccine against this infection makes Ebola an ideal candidate as a biological terror agent. The Ebola virus is transmissible through blood, secretions, and through the air, and can enter the body through skin lesions, mucosa, eyes, etc."

"Can you tell me more about this illness?"

"The name Ebola is derived from the name of the river in the Democratic Republic of the Congo. Again, it is believed, but not fully confirmed, that during the known outbreaks humans obtained the Ebola virus from animals, maybe monkeys or primates. The disease is highly contagious and symptoms include fever, sore throat, diarrhea, dry cough, rash, and internal and external bleeding. It is fatal in fifty to ninety percent of patients and there is no treatment available and no vaccines for prevention. This is what is known from the literature."

"You mentioned before the hybrid virus between Ebola and smallpox. What is this?"

"Here is the focus of my story. Even more dangerous than Ebola is the possibility of an artificially created viral hybrid of Ebola with smallpox called *blackpox* or *Ebolapox*, which is intended to combine bioweapon 'advantages' of both viruses, such as stability in the environment, high infectiveness, high virulence, lethality, and inability for protection by vaccination. The difficulty in creating this hybrid is due to the fact that smallpox virus is a DNA virus, while Ebola is RNA. There were claims by Ken Alibek that the Russian researchers made a DNA copy of an essential part of Ebola's RNA, and then grafted it into the DNA of the smallpox virus. Alibek also claimed that such hybrid has already been developed, but others, such as Sergey Popov, Alibek's former colleague in the Russian program, have recently said that Russian scientists failed in this attempt, and that such technology does not exist, yet. Of course, smallpox, Ebola, and Ebolapox are not the only options among those who are considering bioterror for the future."

"Thank you, Boris, for this story. It is very scary, indeed, and I understand more now about your fears, especially with regard to the knowledge of secrets in the technology of the viral recombination. I feel that you are doing the right thing by exposing these secrets through publication. It may deprive us from certain advantages, but overall it is better for everyone's safety. I think you should share your concerns with police or FBI and seek their advice."

Chapter 10 -

Another Death

The tunnel constructed ten years earlier was to connect the new two-story building containing Genetic Research and Molecular Diagnostic laboratories with the main seven-story building where other laboratories were located. The tunnel was mostly used for getting to and from the parking lot to the workplace and the cafeteria, both of which were located in the main building. For most employees, the workday began at eight A.M. After that time, the tunnel traffic was sparse for the major part of the day. On this particular day in October, the weather in Montana was unusually warm. Wanting to take advantage of the beautiful autumn day, almost everyone chose to walk outside and across the boulevard to reach the main building. Therefore, there was no notice that the security staff blocked the tunnel entrances. At ten-fifteen A.M., two police cars and an ambulance arrived, at which time several police officers entered the tunnel, where they found a corpse!

Rashid Siddiqi, the police inspector, knew the place well from previous events. After instructing the detectives, the medical examiner, and the photographer, he left the crime scene in the tunnel and headed to Mr. Clinton's office.

"Mr. Clinton, I must inform you that we have just found Dr. Dellinger's body in the janitor's closet in the tunnel. However, this time there is no mystery regarding the cause of death. He was shot in the back at close range. We'll know more after the autopsy. We'll investigate further and will keep you informed of our progress. I'm requesting that you not discuss the circumstances of Dr. Dellinger's death until we have an idea who the possible perpetrator might be. We need to contact Dr. Dellinger's wife to come here for formal identification and for some questioning. Please ask your staff to arrange for her to come as soon as possible. Of course, we will need cooperation from your employees during this process, but first I'd like to ask Mrs. Rodrigues how she found the body."

Martha Rodrigues was brought to the Vice President's office by one of the detectives. Although in shock and distraught, she was able to answer the inspector's questions. She said, "I arrived as usual at eight A.M. and began to clean the first floor of the main building. Around ten A.M., I went to the closet in the tunnel where I keep my cleaning supplies to clean the tunnel. The man was lying face down in a pool of blood in a crooked position. I thought that he was either Dr. Dellinger or Dr. Filatov. They look alike from the back. I was sure he was dead. I didn't touch anything. I just closed the door and called the Security Office. That's all."

Mr. Siddiqi said, "Thank you, Mrs. Rodrigues. Please don't discuss with anyone what you have seen or the possible identity of the deceased. You will need to sign this document confirming that you will not discuss this with anyone. You may now return to your work, but please don't enter the tunnel until the policemen finish their work there."

Mr. Clinton said, "Mr. Siddiqi, I don't have to tell you how shocking this is for me personally, not to mention the problem it has created for the institution. Please let me know how I can assist with your investigation."

"First, I would like to use your office, since employees might feel more comfortable here during questioning. I would also like to prepare a list of individuals to question based on their knowledge and interactions with Dr. Dellinger."

That's all that took place in Mr. Clinton's office, and both Mr. Clinton and Mr. Siddiqi realized that a lot of problems were on the horizon.

Murder investigation was not new for Rashid Siddiqi. It was his routine job. What *was* unusual was the setting in which it occurred, and the fact that an important scientist was killed in his workplace, in a respected prominent scientific medical institution.

Born in Pakistan, Rashid grew up in Lebanon in the home of his uncle, a prominent physician. His father was killed in Pakistan when Rashid was fifteen years old. He took an active role in the police investigation of what appeared to be the politically motivated murder of his father by a fanatical religious group. This tragedy triggered Rashid's interest in becoming a detective, but also turned him away from strict religious observance, although he remained religious. His uncle's connections with the king's court helped him to come to the U.S., and he received his education at the Police Academy in the U.S. Now, at age sixty, he had earned a reputation as a very skillful and successful detective among his colleagues, which resulted in promotion to the rank of Inspector.

The first move was to contact the police department in North Brunswick, New Jersey, to do a background check on Dellinger for any criminal record or any conflicts that could have led to his murder. According to the report by the medical examiner, the autopsy confirmed the cause of death as a shot at close range with a 12-gauge handgun, perhaps with a silencer. The bullet entered the chest from the back and penetrated the heart. The inspector realized that information collected previously by him and by the FBI agents regarding the interaction among the employees of this institution could be useful. He began by interviewing some of the directors and those who had ongoing contact with Dr. Dellinger.

Despite several days of interviews, none had yielded any possible suspect. Although Siddiqi knew about Rebecca Brown's problems with Dellinger, her defensive and nervous demeanor during the interview aroused his curiosity. He would have another conversation with her.

Martha Trump, Dr. Dellinger's girlfriend, was brought to the police headquarters, where she was informed of his death by Rashid Siddiqi. Her shock was evidenced by the pale appearance of her countenance. For a while, she sat completely silent. Before questioning her, Siddiqi offered her a cup of tea while she recovered from the shocking news.

"Ms. Trump, I have some questions to ask, however, if you don't feel up to talking now, we can talk later. In any case, I must take you to the morgue for the formal identification of Dr. Dellinger."

"I am fine now, and we can talk. We can go to the morgue afterwards."

"Do you have any idea who would want to kill Dr. Dellinger?"

At this point, I am unable to think of anyone who would want to do such a horrible thing; however, I will give it some additional thought and let you know if I come up with anyone. Jim confessed to me that he had a very complicated relationship with his wife and there were also other women in his life when he lived in New Jersey. I didn't care to know the sordid details. When we first met, Jim immediately impressed me and I fell in love with him. I thought that he had changed and would be faithful to me. He treated me very well, and eventually we planned to marry, but his wife kept putting obstacles in the way of their divorce. We lived separately, and recently our relationship started to cool. I even started suspecting that Jim was attracted to another woman."

"Thank you, Ms. Trump. I would ask you to keep Dr. Dellinger's death secret for the time being. We will preserve his body properly until the official announcement of his death is made. I'm sorry for all the suffering you have to go through. Again, please call me if you can provide me the names of any suspects."

The next interview was held in Mr. Clinton's office with Dr. Gupta.

"Dr. Gupta, I must inform you that Dr. Dellinger was killed, and I am asking you to keep this information secret until the official announcement. What are your thoughts in regard to the fact that Dr. Dellinger was killed in the tunnel connecting the main building and the one where only two laboratories are located, yours and the Genetics Research Laboratory? Did he visit these laboratories often?"

"I can say that he did not have any special interest in my laboratory until we began testing the samples from Dr. Meyer's body. Surprisingly, he had been coming to the genetics laboratory at least three times a week, always in the morning."

"Why surprisingly?"

"Because it's not a diagnostic, but research laboratory, and only formally included in the Department of Diagnostic Laboratories. Originally, Dr. Sandoval reported directly to Mr. Clinton, but that recently changed when Mr. Clinton assigned Dr. Dellinger to oversee the genetic laboratory's interaction with the 'Company' regarding the contract that was established between the 'Company' and the Institute."

"Is this the reason and the only reason for these frequent visits and what seems to be kind of an increased interest by Dr. Dellinger?"

"It may be, but his increased interest, as you said, is understandable because in addition to the contract with the 'Company,' Dr. Sandoval has been working on a subject that is very important for the future of gene therapy. As I understand it, Dr. Dellinger wanted to be a part of accreditation, patenting, and related to its potentially great future."

"Do you think that he had essential qualifications to contribute to the progress of this research?"

"I don't think so, but that is my personal impression and I don't know any details of his involvement. After all, he had a significant amount of administrative and financial authorities to aid in the progress of this study."

"Did Dr. Sandoval welcome Dr. Dellinger's involvement in this project, even though it was beyond the contract with the 'Company,' which was an issue to be officially monitored by Dr. Dellinger?"

"At the beginning, she was very reluctant to even discuss this issue with Dr. Dellinger, and he suspected, as I observed during our group meetings, that she was hiding something about the progress in her research. I believe that the situation changed recently. I noticed quite friendly personal interactions between them. Maybe it has nothing to do with the research. After all, Dr. Dellinger was a very attractive man, and Maryann has been lonely since her separation from her husband."

"You mean possibly a romantic involvement along with the professional interactions?"

"I don't know, the whole situation is quite complicated. You see, I knew Maryann and her husband, Sam Sandoval, for a long time before I came to work here. They used to work together somewhere else. He is an exceptional virologist and, perhaps, together they had some success in developing tools that are important for gene therapy, but they stopped collaborating after their separation. Before their separation, he was quite jealous when she paid attention to other men and seemed tormented by her indifference toward him. Perhaps, he is still in love with her, but that's just my guess."

"Final question, Dr. Gupta. Genetic research is a highly competitive field. Is it possible that jealousy among the other scientists could be a factor in Dr. Dellinger's death?"

"I cannot imagine such a scenario. I don't know of any such thing happening in the research community, although hatred may not be foreign to some scientists. They are human beings, after all. Nevertheless, with so many people involved in research, I would not completely exclude that possibility."

"Any other ideas or possibilities, no matter how wild?"

"Just one really wild thought. You know, some of the genetic research, especially the genetic manipulation of the viruses, might be of interest to the military, taking into account the well-known use of these and similar developments in the former Soviet Union regarding biological warfare agents. Numerous publications have documented that our institution is involved in sophisticated genetic studies. Surprisingly, the U.S. agencies responsible for protection against such forms of war have never contacted our institution, but perhaps some foreign groups might have."

"You mean an interest in sophisticated procedures of viral genetic manipulations developed at this institution?"

"Yes, but it's a wild guess, as you said. Just a thought after reading publications by Ken Alibek, the biological warfare expert that defected from Russia."

"Well, these are interesting thoughts, maybe not so wild and, perhaps, useful to pursue. Thank you, Dr. Gupta."

Siddiqi had known for a long time that science was far from being an "ivory tower," but he was surprised to learn the extent of sinister machinations in such a noble field. With this in mind, he decided to broaden his investigation to include the possibility of professional jealousy, 'murder by scientist.'

Dr. Sandoval was next in line for Siddiqi to interview.

"Dr. Sandoval, are you satisfied with the progress of your research since Dr. Filatov joined your team, and how helpful was Dr. Dellinger with your project?"

"It is going along fine, especially after Dr. Filatov was assigned to help me. I'm confused; why are the police interested in this research?"

"Dr. Sandoval, there has been a tragedy. Dr. Dellinger was killed, and we don't know who may have done it, or why. So, we are searching for any clues or information regarding his activities. In order to conduct a successful investigation we must, at this time, keep his death secret. Therefore, I am asking you not to speak to anyone about his death. May I ask you few questions related to Dr. Dellinger's recent activities, or we can continue our conversation later?"

"It's a shock for me, but we can talk now."

"Dr. Dellinger was killed yesterday in the tunnel, between nine and ten A.M. Did he visit your laboratory before nine A.M., or was he planning to come later?"

"He usually visited my laboratory in the morning and I was surprised that he didn't come yesterday."

"I understand he visited systematically. What was the purpose of these visits?"

"The primary purpose was to monitor our collaboration with the company that contributed to the establishment of my laboratory. We have an obligation to report the progress of this research, and Dr. Dellinger was in charge of preparing these monthly reports."

"Was he involved in other projects, in particular the one that you are conducting with Dr. Filatov? If so, what was Dr. Dellinger's role?"

"The project you are talking about, development of alternative methods for gene therapy has not been funded by the 'Company.' Dr. Dellinger's involvement has been instrumental in arranging private funds for this study. He obviously wanted to be a formal participant in the study, and, if it is successful, he would have received all the credit and benefits."

"Is your ex-husband still involved with you in this project?"

"First of all, our divorce isn't final, so he is not yet my 'ex.' There isn't any significant reason. Sam just keeps asking for postponements because he still hopes that we can get back together. He is now performing completely different research related to the diagnostic methods for various viral infections, a project funded by an NIH grant. He's no longer involved in my research, but he sometimes visits me in the laboratory. I believe scientific issues are only an excuse. He comes for personal reasons."

"Do you think he's angry or jealous that someone else is taking advantage of his past collaboration with you in the development of certain systems for gene transportation?"

"I don't think so. After all, the past achievements were not so great, and not much different from results by other scientific groups."

"Has he ever met with Dr. Filatov or Dr. Dellinger?"

"No, not even once."

"What are your thoughts about Dr. Dellinger's murder? Did he have any enemies at the institution or elsewhere? Why would someone want him dead?"

"I am shocked! I can't think of anyone that would have reason to kill Dr. Dellinger."

"Is it possible that an outside group would be engaged in such sinister application, perhaps developing biological warfare agents, using this technology, and then use Dr. Dellinger to gain access to your secrets?"

"First, I don't think that we have exclusive knowledge in the area of genetic engineering of the viruses and, second, why would anyone want to kill someone who obviously is not the top expert in this field? What is there to gain by killing Dr. Dellinger? I don't think there is any validity in such a scenario."

"Thank you, Dr. Sandoval. Please keep our conversation secret, as well as the death of Dr. Dellinger."

Siddiqi had two reasons for requesting an interview with Dr. Filatov. First, according to Mrs. Brown, Filatov often met with Dellinger while working in the Microbiology Laboratory and she often saw them together in the cafeteria and in other places. In addition, Siddiqi started seriously pondering the possibility of what he began referring to as 'a sinister application of the genetic studies.'

"Dr. Filatov, although it has not yet been publicized, you've no doubt heard that Dr. Dellinger is dead, and I'm asking you to honor this stance, at least outside of this institution. I understand that you and Dr. Dellinger met quite often. Did he ever indicate that he was afraid someone was out to get him?"

"I don't think so. We talked only about the progress of my research with genetic manipulations of viruses, the project that Dr. Sandoval conducts. He obviously did not have sufficient background to understand either my work with viruses, or the general issues of therapeutic gene transportation. Frankly, I was surprised by his enormous interest in these issues."

"As I was told, perhaps Dr. Dellinger wanted to be part of a very promising project, which would greatly benefit him if it were successful."

"Yes, definitely! Sometimes he would violate ethics by asking me to get information from Dr. Sandoval's laboratory that he suspected she was hiding from him. We did have an unpleasant conversation about that issue. Afterwards, he quit trying to push me around, either because of our conversation or maybe because he and Dr. Sandoval became very friendly. But now, I don't believe she did hide anything from him."

"May I ask you to explain these potential secrets? Are there meaningful and possible secrets in your type of research?"

"Yes, very much so. Development of gene therapy is a very complicated issue, but let me limit it to one issue, just to answer your questions. One part of this research is to develop vehicles to deliver the so-called therapeutic gene into the human body. One type of such vector can be a virus that must be modified — or as it is called, genetically engineered — to serve this purpose effectively and, at the same time, be harmless. That's my part of work in the project. Dr. Sandoval handles the rest of it. Possessing such viruses and how you are developing them can be a great secret because it may result in patenting and huge benefits, along with scientific honors for important discoveries."

"Do you think Dr. Dellinger suspected that Dr. Sandoval was successful in developing such viruses? How would his suspicion be justified, since Dr. Sandoval is not a virologist skillful in genetic engineering of the viruses?"

"You're absolutely right, but he knew that Dr. Sandoval worked in the past with her husband, who is a very knowledgeable and skillful virologist. I understand their collaboration stopped after their separation."

"Do you think she may be in possession of such viruses?"

"I don't know, but it's very unlikely. She told me that success appeared to be close, but not yet complete, and she gave me all the viral strains with which she was working."

"How successful are you, so far?"

"I'm optimistic. I am using quite sophisticated technology based on making hybrids of viruses that combine a desirable combination of features inherited from the original viral strains involved. I learned some of this technology from my father back in Russia when he was working on the development of some vaccines. In fact, involvement in vaccine development and related genetic manipulation technology was the major reason my father wanted me to emigrate and never go back. Keep in mind that making viral hybrids is not only for noble reasons like vaccine development or gene therapy, but also may well be used for evil purposes like creating a 'perfect biological weapon.' One example is an attempt to create hybrids between Ebola and smallpox viruses. There were rumors that development of such hybrids was done in a super-secret institution in

Siberia. Although my father was not involved in such work, he feared that some people in the Russian military or security leadership might come across my training skills and recruit me for this type of work, which my father was against."

"Thank you for telling me about it. Of course, I will keep it confidential. Your explanations are very helpful, and I thank you for your openness. I wish you the best in your research. Sometime in the near future, I would like to know more about the chilling issue of the viral hybrids intended for the biological warfare."

"You can read about this issue in books and interviews by Ken Alibek, the scientist who defected to the U.S. from the Soviet Union. He was the administrator in charge of the biological warfare program.

"My father was not involved in any of these programs, but creation of the vaccines against some viral infections requires sophisticated skills in manipulation between DNA and RNA, and in creating some viral hybrids. He kept a very low profile regarding his skills, some of which he shared with me informally, although he never allowed my official involvement in his projects. He also told me that I should attempt to publish this information if I was involved in any viral recombination experiments in the U.S. He called it 'life security.'"

"Are you following your father's advice?"

"Definitely…although I have not yet achieved the desirable success in creating virus strains that would be harmless to humans and serve effectively in the gene transport. I believe that I am very close to it. So far, I have submitted a paper for publication on methodology for creating viral hybrids with a desirable combination of features, and *Nature* will publish it next month! So, there will be no dangerous secrets for which to hunt me."

"Congratulations! So, it seems that you have protected yourself well. Nevertheless, I am thinking more and more that killing Dr. Dellinger might be part of a foreign conspiracy. I don't want to frighten you, but you should know that they may have had killing you in mind, but mistook Dr. Dellinger for you; from the back, you and he look very similar. Since we have not yet reported Dr.

Dellinger's death, I would like to place you in protective custody for a few days to confuse the killer and his bosses, if my theory is correct. Would you accept the offer to stay in our protective custody for a few days in a very nice place out of the city?"

"I'm not afraid. My father predicted such a possibility, and it may appear that he was right. Of course, I agree."

"Then don't go to your office. Go home and wait until I make the necessary arrangements. The official explanation for your absence will be that you went to a scientific conference in New York City. I will make the same offer to Dr. Sandoval. Thank you for your cooperation, and good luck!"

Chapter 11 -

In Moscow

Special Tasks, a sensational book published in 1994 by Little, Brown and Company, describes activities of the Soviet intelligence service's elite unit. The author of this book was Pavel Sudoplatov (in collaboration with his son Anatoli), the former head of this Administration for Special Tasks. The book describes in detail that in addition to espionage, the major goal of the Administration for Special Tasks was assassinations, mostly abroad. It was unknown prior to publication of this book that such an organization existed.

According to the listings currently posted by the Russian government, no such agency exists in the modern Russian Federation, and one could assume that its former employees are either dead or unemployed. Nevertheless, some media reports claim, '...the Kremlin has a nasty record of eliminating its enemies abroad...,' referring to a series of deaths of exiled Russians in England. For example, one is the report by Luke Harding published in *The Guardian* on March 23, 2013. The report states that Scotland Yard believes that in 2006, two former Russian KGB officers, Lugovoi and Kovtun, poisoned Litvinenko, a former KGB Russian agent living in exile, with polonium-210, and this episode may have affected relations between

Russia and the U.K. According to Boris Karpichkov, a former KGB agent who defected to the U.K., the FSB, the current name of the former KGB, has a great number of clandestine methods for murder, for example, an odorless substance called sodium fluoride. He also said that some colorless, odorless, lethal substances can be applied to personal items and are not detectable in a postmortem examination. So, the question remains unanswered as to whether any of the agencies, or semi-official groups of the Russian Federation, could be involved in any assassinations abroad. This possibility cannot be excluded. Some reports point to the existence of poison laboratories headquartered in Yasenevo, near Moscow, that are in charge of developing sophisticated poisons intended for assassinations, as referred to in a publication by A. Kouzminov, *Biological Espionage,* Greenhill Books, 2006.

Foreign tourists walking the peaceful streets of Moscow would not even think about the possibility of the existence of an organization such as Special Tasks, but the perception was no different in the past when Special Tasks did exist. After all, such organizations do not hang their signs on the entrance of their buildings.

Not only is Moscow the capital and the largest city in Russia, with a population of more than 11.5 million, it is in many ways unique and different from the rest of Russia. It is Europe's most expensive city and has the largest number of billionaires, although the average monthly income of Moscow residents is less than nine hundred dollars per month. Moscow is an eclectic city, in which the architectural elements are similar to that in any European capital combined with remnants of Stalin-era neo-gothic skyscrapers in the central parts of the city and rather unattractive, even ugly apartment buildings on the periphery. In addition, there are several modern-style hotels recently constructed by international companies alongside the old Soviet-era buildings. The eclecticism of the city is not just in the architecture. It is in the uniqueness of the general atmosphere, which is often shocking to the foreigners. The streets are overcrowded with cars, a large proportion of which are expensive foreign models, but the driving style is extremely aggressive and chaotic, and drivers don't respect or demonstrate even minimal attention to the safety of pedestrians. The stores are filled with a variety of goods, but the salesclerks are rather hostile, as described in the literature in the style of the Soviet-era salespeople. People in the streets and those traveling in the subway are well dressed, but it is remarkable how carefully and skillfully they avoid any eye contact, and they never smile if such contact occurs, and would never say, "Hello," to a stranger. The 'neutral' or rather gloomy facial expression dominates, which is perceived by many foreign visitors as unfriendliness.

In recent years, life in Moscow, St. Petersburg, and a few other major cities in Russia has become economically, culturally, and socially quite active, but not so in the rest of the country. Nevertheless, many Russians, regardless of where they reside, often express pride in the new developments in Moscow and Russia, in general, by referring to a greater freedom of speech than was allowed under the Soviet Union regime, and to the number of political parties that are fighting for power. Also, they refer to the openness or 'transparency,' as some American politicians would call it, and not having any of shadowy agencies of the past. Yet, there are two questions that remain. Is it true that Russia is no longer involved in subversive activities abroad? Is it true that Russia is no longer involved in the development of biological warfare?

There are many restaurants and clubs in areas like Arbat. There are also places that appear to be restaurants on the surface. If anyone tried to enter one of these places believing it to be a restaurant, a few burly men in the lobby would let them know that it was a private club and ask the 'invader' to leave. These places may be private clubs, such as the notorious 'patriotic' organization called Pamyat, but they also may be government offices, which were not indicated on the entrance. The Arbat district, one of the oldest historic parts of the city, is full of such unmarked places. Some of them are in by-streets, situated in small old buildings that were once the private houses of nobility or wealthy merchants before the October Revolution.

November is usually very cold in Moscow, but the streets of the city are usually crowded in any season. Many people walk from one of their places of employment to another or taking 'breaks.' Groups of foreign tourists can be seen in some specific areas in central parts of the city.

One would not distinguish some individuals wearing warm civilian clothes like everybody else, walking to a special small gathering at the unmarked small building in one of the Arbat area by-streets.

A group of men started gathering in one such small old building that had survived the recent modernization of the famous Arbat Street. Although they were in plain clothes, judging by their posture and the way they walked one might notice that some of them may have been military men. Among a number of important places located in this area is the Ministry of Defense main building, and down the road at Smolenskaya Square is the Ministry of Foreign Affairs. The leading individuals of these organizations often had important small meetings intended as 'conversations' without any formal records, outside of their headquarters, but within walking distance from their offices.

This was not the first meeting of this group, and they all were familiar with each other. In traditional Russia style, they addressed each other by the first name with patronymic, without mentioning rank or the last name. They knew which organization or group each of them represented, whether listed or not listed in certain directories. One characteristic of these men was that they all had a rather 'blank' facial expression with no distinct features and showing no emotions.

They sat at a long table, and Vasily Ivanovitch, the tallest man in the group, took his place at the head of the table as chairman. He directed his first question to the person sitting at his right. "Vladimir Petrovitch, please give this group a perspective on the happening in Greeneville."

"It all started with the cancellation of research on the recombination of viruses of Marburg plus smallpox and Ebola plus smallpox at the Vector Institute in Siberia, when Americans from the Division of Nonproliferation at the U.S. State Department were allowed to visit that place. At the time, our explanation for working with these viruses was that we were developing vaccines against these infections, and we never admitted to any attempts to create hybrids among those viruses. In fact, these attempts failed, and after two people at Vector Institute died from Ebola, we really stopped all work of this type. Later, we learned that Dr. Dmitry Filatov, working at the Moscow University, had developed a new methodology for making viral hybrids while working on various vaccines, such as those against viral meningitis, hepatitis types A, B, and C, against mumps, HIV, tumors, etc. Some attempts were successful, but some were not. In the past, he declined our offers to work for us, and with the new developments, we were concerned that his technology was exactly what we tried to achieve in the past at the Vector Institute. He died in 2011, and none of his studies were finished and published. So, there wasn't concern that Americans or other countries would obtain information about the viral recombination technology. We influenced the group at the Moscow University to ban any further research on viral recombinants. That is until we learned that Dr. Dmitry Filatov's son, Boris, who immigrated to the U.S. with his father's help, is using the same technology for development of the therapy in Montana's institute."

Chairman Vasily Ivanovitch, said, "Vladimir Petrovitch, how can you explain that Boris Filatov, with this knowledge and expertise, could escape our attention and begin using his knowledge in the U.S.?"

"First of all, Boris Filatov never participated in his father's research, so no one was aware of his expertise in viral recombination. He received training as a molecular biologist and virologist during his fellowship at the Medical School and, therefore, was not among individuals on our watch list. Perhaps his father did not want him to be formally involved in the type of research that we are discussing. So, he quietly made Boris emigrate to the U.S. under the guise of further training. Boris has never come back to Moscow, not even for his father's funeral. It was unexpected that he suddenly began working on viral recombinants, using the technological information that he, perhaps, verbally obtained from his father, and is now combining it with new knowledge from training in the U.S."

"How do you know that he is doing the type of research that is of concern to us?"

"Through our consultant at the Moscow University, we contacted our man, a molecular biologist in New York. We asked him to get in touch with Boris at the scientific conference under the pretense of a scientific discussion. Boris did not show any caution and revealed information confirming our awareness obtained previously through the same person. The information was double checked — it was accurate."

"I think it's sloppiness, although I understand that it's difficult to keep secret some scientific knowledge that may have a broad application in a number of fields. Nevertheless, we must keep such knowledge from being passed on to the U.S. Army Medical Command installation in Fort Detrick, National Interagency Confederation for Biological Research (NICBR), and other similar U.S. institutions."

"I understand, Vasily Ivanovitch, but we have done what is within our power to fix the problem, and the only option we had to prevent the spread of information was to eliminate Boris Filatov."

The chairman looked around and asked, "Who can explain why such a primitive method, a gun, was used, while to the best of my knowledge your department has developed so many new tools that are untraceable?"

Vladimir Petrovitch raised his hand and said, after Vasily Ivanovitch nodded his head, "We were instructed that the methods you mention became a signature of Russian activity after they were widely used in England. Using a gun would make an impression and create suspicion that it was possibly a local deal with no political motives, but rather for personal reason, such as revenge, competition, jealousy over a woman, or something similar."

Vasily Ivanovitch said, "That was a good strategy, but did it work and why was your man sent from New York? Didn't you have somebody locally?"

Vladimir Petrovitch said, "Sergei Michailovitch managed this operation and can better answer your question. Sergei Michailovitch, please."

"Greeneville is a new small city and we don't have anyone there. In the past, we had someone in Helena, the capital of Montana, but that person, a former police officer, is now too old to handle such a task, and has retired. However, we were able to use him this time. The day before the planned action, he delivered a package with a Beretta and a silencer to a coded box in the airport. The man who came from New York is familiar with the place, since he works for the company that inspects the autoclaves that are under contract in many medical institutions, and his appearance at the Institute, if noticed, would not be surprising. This man, James, was properly instructed concerning Boris. James came to Greeneville early in the morning and set up his target at the anticipated position. Perhaps, he inspected some autoclaves, and then left for New York at noon. The mission was accomplished, but for some strange reason, there has been no report of the death of Boris Filatov by the authorities."

The meeting adjourned, and Vasily Ivanovitch suggested, "Let's meet tomorrow at ten in the morning, if we receive new information."

The only source for new information of Boris's death they could expect would be through the media or through a person at the Moscow University who had to contact someone in New York. There was still no announcement on the next day or even in the following two weeks, nor was there information from other sources. The only reason for another meeting was the appearance of Boris's publication in *Nature* outlining the technology of viral recombination for creating new hybrids as vehicles for therapeutic gene delivery and for development of live vaccines.

The chairman summoned only five people of the group to the next meeting. Chairman Vasily Ivanovitch said, "So far, we don't know whether Boris Filatov is alive or dead, but it does not matter now. His recent publication in *Nature* makes public knowledge of all the secrets. We failed to prevent it, and now our scientists can learn the technology from this publication. It seems that Boris Filatov was following instructions from his late father to protect himself, but it was too late. On the other hand, we should forget about him if he is still alive and not to pursue his elimination. It makes no sense anymore. Vladimir Petrovitch, did your people check with your man in New York about the events in Greeneville?"

"Yes, we did. Our man, James, actually saw the police team remove the body from the tunnel and load it into the ambulance. Afterwards, no one noticed him and he didn't go to check the autoclaves as previously planned, but left the premises. He safely arrived in New York and was not followed. We have been unable to reach him, and recently learned from his employer's records that he left for vacation."

Vasily Ivanovitch shrugged and said, "I don't like it. Something is wrong, and I sense trouble. Vladimir Petrovitch and Sergey Michailovitch, your man James made a mistake by not checking at any medical institution to justify his trip to Greeneville. I want to bring him to Moscow. I'm afraid he would 'sing' if he's captured by the Americans. What is your plan?"

Vladimir Petrovitch said, "As you've asked before, I checked various options and the feasibility of the following. James will begin dating a woman of Mexican origin that speaks Spanish, and he will take a vacation with her to California. From San Diego, they will take a bus tour to Tijuana in Mexico. This five-hour round-trip is available on Thursday and Sunday starting at two P.M. In Tijuana, at the end of the tour, they will tell the tour guide they want to stay overnight in Tijuana according to the prior reservation and such a reservation will be arranged. They will check in, but will not actually stay in the hotel. They will take the pre-arranged taxi at the hotel, and drive to the local airport for a flight to Mexico City. There they will go to the Aeroflot office for a flight to Moscow."

"That's a reasonable plan, if it works. First you have to find him, but I am afraid it may be already too late."

His premonition was correct. As seen in the papers, Boris gave his presentation, based on his published report, at the scientific conference in New York as he had planned. More bad news for Vasily Ivanovitch was yet to come....

Chapter 12 -

Indentified and Arrested

From his experience and after reviewing all the conversations he had before, Siddiqi got the feeling that the perpetrator was not among the employees of the Institute or even local. Two of his detectives continued observation and surveillance of a few local individuals, but he did not have much hope for any positive outcome. The death of Dr. Dellinger continued to be a secret, and a rumor was spread that he and Dr. Filatov left town for a scientific conference and subsequent vacations. The discussion with Boris Filatov gave Siddiqi a strong feeling for the need to pursue the hypothesis of foreign involvement. He could not do it alone and contacted his old friend Andrew Powell at the FBI. Of course, it was a wild guess, but together they developed a plan. First, they set up investigation to analyze the individuals who were not local residents, but had visited Greeneville during the two days before and the day of the murder.

Montana has several airports, with eight of them being international. Siddiqi and Powell started the investigation with airports located within reasonable driving distance to Greeneville from the southwestern corner of the state: Bozeman, Billings, Dillon, and Livingston. Even after excluding those whose profile did not fit the perpetrator's, the detectives were assigned to search through a long list. In addition, the search included hotel registers. Eventually, they narrowed down the list to twelve individuals who came from New York, Philadelphia, or Los Angeles. Investigation of these twelve would include their background, character, interactions, and their activities during the days in question.

This tedious work continued for three days, until they came across the inexplicable behavior of a person who used to inspect the autoclaves at the medical institutions. He arrived from New York in the morning and left at noon, but he did not go to any of the hospitals, to the University in Bozeman, or to the Institute in Greeneville. His name was Patrick McMahon, the son of Irish immigrants. He had no criminal record, and he had a good reputation at his place of employment. He was immediately placed under surveillance, and the regional FBI office obtained the authority to place him on the Do Not Board (DNB) federal list for any foreign flight. The Centers for Disease Control and Prevention (CDC) created the DNB list to prevent travel by individuals who have active tuberculosis or some other infectious diseases. However, it became a convenient tool for use by other agencies, as well. That is, in addition to the 'Secure Flight'" and other similar systems intended for better control of passengers departing from the U.S. Mr. Powell thought that now he had enough information to pass the file to the FBI headquarters in Washington and a group of special agents would continue the investigation.

The very first piece of information obtained by the group was that Mr. McMahon had traveled to many places in the U.S. as part of his job, but had never traveled abroad. So far, his behavior did not indicate anything suspicious and there were no reasons or excuses to bring him in for interrogation. Approaching Mr. McMahon without any evidence that he had committed a crime, suspicious activity, or contact with a foreign agent, would yield no results. The surveillance was tough and close, but nothing suspicious appeared. McMahon was a loner, did not have any friends, and was not involved with women, except an occasional date. He did not have any hobbies, except watching football and basketball games, and reading lots of books.

This suddenly changed. Mr. McMahon began dating a woman, a naturalized American citizen by the name Maria Gonzales. Ms. Gonzalez came from Mexico seven years earlier and, since then, had been on the FBI watch list for suspicious contact with drug dealers. She started spending nights at McMahon's place, and often they went out to restaurants or to the movies. McMahon continued to travel quite often, always on business.

One of the FBI special agents, Mark Griffin, was a former student at the Academy of Art University with the hopes of one day becoming an actor. Eventually, he changed his mind and began a career at the FBI, but was still fascinated with his ability to change his appearance. This skill became very useful in his surveillance work. He now applied it while closely observing Mr. McMahon's activities and that was not an easy task, taking into account his frequent short visits to medical institutions in different cities.

Mark realized that McMahon must have been receiving instructions, if indeed he was really a foreign agent, and finding those contacts would be a top priority. McMahon's cell phone record indicated that all his calls were about making arrangements with clients or his office when traveling, and did not reveal anything suspicious. He did not use Skype as a means of communication with his clients. Mark knew that professional criminals would be cautious about using phones, and, perhaps, would communicate only in person by special arrangement. Therefore, he took on the difficult task of following McMahon to the cities that he visited professionally, each time changing his appearance or 'function' at different places, such as pretending to be a medical person, electrician, or plumber. Following McMahon, a man in his mid-30s, was not difficult technically, although he did not have an extraordinary appearance or features — middle height, unimpressive face, gray eyes, and most often dressed casually. One occasion attracted Mark's attention. During McMahon's visits to the University Hospital of Brooklyn, he would go to the cafeteria to have tea and meet with one of the employees, Mr. Edward Hilton, a technologist at the diagnostic laboratories. Perhaps, it didn't mean anything, but McMahon and Hilton met several times. Mark put Hilton under surveillance, but nothing out of the ordinary happened.

Other developments did not escape Mark's attention. McMahon purchased two tickets to San Francisco with a tour of Southern California. He did not arrange a tour from San Diego to Mexico, but Mark knew that a tour to Tijuana from San Diego could be done without prior reservations. Traveling via Mexico might obviate precautions that were set up to prevent McMahon from leaving the country via U.S. airports. It would be difficult to catch him in Mexico and, without any clear evidence that he committed a crime, the Mexican authorities would not cooperate, and nothing would prevent him from boarding an international flight from there. It was imperative to detain and interrogated him on U.S. soil! The FBI could prevent him from flying to California, but interference with his travel could alarm him and could spoil any further investigation. A legitimate reason was necessary to explain his possible retention in the U.S.

The situation changed — an agreement between the U.S. and Mexican foreign affairs authorities was reached to arrest McMahon in Mexico if he attempted to board a flight to any place other than the U.S. This would provide clear evidence of his possible illegal activities, giving FBI sufficient reason to detain him for interrogation.

As expected, McMahon and Maria Gonzales made a reservation from their hotel in San Francisco for a tour from San Diego to Tijuana, arrived by bus to San Diego early Sunday morning, and boarded the tour bus at two P.M. Mark Griffin closely followed the bus in an unmarked car, and then followed the tour group on foot in Tijuana. At the end of the tour, Mark stayed close to the group and overheard the couple tell the guide they would stay at Hotel Lucerna in Tijuana for one night, according to their prior reservation, and return the next day on their own. The guide argued with them, saying that it was his responsibility to bring the group back to the U.S., but he finally relented and took a note from them to deliver to the border patrol. McMahon and Maria checked into the hotel, but soon walked out and left in a taxicab. When Mark realized the taxi was taking the couple to the international airport near Tijuana, he called his office to make further arrangements, and followed them to the aircraft for the flight to Mexico City. Upon arrival in Mexico City, a local man greeted Maria with a hug. Maria introduced her friend to McMahon and they shook hands. After a while, both men went to the men's room, after which Maria and the stranger left. McMahon went to the waiting area for boarding international flights, including the Russian Aeroflot, where he made himself comfortable in a soft chair and began reading his book. Mark was thinking that, perhaps, the stranger gave McMahon the ticket and other documents when they went to the restroom.

The next flight to Moscow was in four hours, but the time was ripe for action. About one hour after Mark made the call, a local uniformed police officer approached McMahon and inquired, "Señor, I noticed that you have been sitting here for a long time, while many flights have departed. Are you waiting for your flight in the right place? May I look at your ticket and your passport?"

"Yes, of course, here are my documents. I think I am in the right place. I just came too early."

"Yes, Señor, you are at the right place, and you may consider going upstairs for lunch. Here are your documents, gracias."

McMahon followed the advice, went upstairs for a snack, and when he came back he saw the same police officer. The officer approached him and said, "Señor, I was looking for you. Someone from the airline wanted to speak with you. Please follow me to their office."

The officer took him through a chain of rooms to a place that seemed far away from the waiting area. McMahon started getting worried, but he did not have any other choice but to follow. At the entrance to a distant room, a man who represented himself as a flight attendant asked in a typical New York accent, "May I see your passport and ticket?" After looking at the documents he asked, "Sir, is the name on your passport and the ticket, Ronald Greenberg, your correct name?"

At this moment, McMahon realized he was trapped, and there were no options to escape, as two men holding him tightly placed cuffs on his hands. At this time, Mark Griffin appeared from the next room and said, "Mr. McMahon, you are not Ronald Greenberg. You are now in a facility that belongs to the U.S. consulate. I am FBI Special Agent Mark Griffin and I've been given authority to take you into custody. You have the right to remain silent. Anything you say can and will be used against you in a court of law. You have the right to an attorney during interrogation; if you cannot afford an attorney, one will be appointed to you. Do you understand your rights?" Then Mexican officials and two guards escorted Agent Griffin and Mr. McMahon to the pre-arranged U.S. aircraft.

After they left, an easel with colorful advertisements of Mexican tours was moved away from the waiting area of the airport. This easel had blocked the view of the entrance to the room where McMahon was taken. The obscured sign near the entrance read, TO THE UNITED STATES CONSULATE.

After repetition of the formal arrest procedure upon arrival to New York, McMahon was placed in a special FBI facility. Interrogation by Mr. William Morton, the police inspector, began immediately after the formalities, including identification, home address statement, employment, etc., were completed.

Mr. Morton said, "Mr. McMahon, what was the reason for replacement of your passport with a false one with a different name and a Russian visa, and who did all this for you?"

"I always wanted to visit Russia, but could not afford to, and this time I was offered the opportunity to go on my dream tour for a very cheap price if I accepted an offer to travel under an assumed name. Maria's close friend made this offer. He is traveling to Russia on business. He knows Russian, but needed someone who knows English well to help him prepare business documents. He was even going to pay me for this work, which made the plan quite attractive. I understand that I made a big mistake to go for that, and I am very sorry."

"So, with this explanation, were you trying to escape from the U.S.? Why? Have you committed a crime? Maybe killed somebody?"

"No, no! My ticket was for a round trip, and I was going to come back to Mexico in a week, which would be within my vacation plans, then Maria and I would return to New York."

"All right, that is enough of telling us your fairytales. You will have to tell us the true story, because we already know the truth anyway. Your future can become terrible if you don't cooperate and don't provide a full confession. We do have evidence that you're a Russian agent, and it will not be to your benefit to continue to deny this fact. The first question is who was the contact who gave you instructions on how to escape from the U.S.?"

"I don't understand what you are talking about. I am not a Russian agent! All of this is ridiculous."

The inspector made a short call and then said, "Someone has already confessed and will be the first among the witnesses of your crime."

The door opened and Edward Hilton, the technician from the Brooklyn hospital, stepped in accompanied by a guard.

"Mr. Hilton, is this the person to whom you passed messages that you received from a source at the Moscow University? How did you handle these messages?"

"The messages were coded via emails BCC'd to me with a confusing address. Usually, they went to my junk mail. I decoded the emails, and typed the decoded message in fluent English using a typewriter just before the scheduled meeting with Mr. McMahon. We would 'accidentally' meet in the cafeteria and have tea at the same table, then I would slip the typewritten paper to Mr. McMahon."

"Do you remember the assignment given to Mr. McMahon?"

"Of course! His assignment was to kill Dr. Filatov, and it contained many details on how to do it."

The inspector stopped him with a gesture and waved to the guard to take Hilton away, and after they left said, "So, Mr. McMahon, we have more witnesses, and the question is whether you are going to talk now or later? By the way, Dr. Filatov is not dead. He is alive and well, which means that you did not fulfill your assignment from the Russians to kill him. We considered allowing you to go to

Russia as a part of an exchange program with the Russian government, but I don't have to tell you the fate there of someone who doesn't fulfill his assignment. On the other hand, there are considerably better options for your future here in the U.S. New York doesn't have the death penalty. A full confession, including the murder of someone who, by the way was not Dr. Filatov, and all the details about the Russian's network in the U.S. will influence the sentence you could receive. Don't answer me now. You will have one hour alone to think it over; after that I will expect your answer."

As expected, McMahon agreed to give his full confession, and was appointed a lawyer to consult the terms of his confession and details regarding his future. McMahon's arrest and confessions helped to find several Russian agents in the U.S., including a few families living in the U.S. with false identities. So far, these sleepers had not committed any crimes and were sent back to Russia as a part of an exchange between the U.S. and Russia. As a result, high-level negotiations between the U.S. and Russia took place, and very strict arrangements were made to cease work on biological weapons by any official or non-official entities.

The conclusion of the murder case brought some relief to everyone affected by it. Mrs. Maria Dellinger requested that her husband's body be released to her for a funeral in New Jersey. The Institute's representatives attended the funeral, and Dr. Dellinger's obituary appeared in newspapers in both places — North Brunswick and Greeneville — describing his life and contribution to science, but it did not mention the cause of death. His friend Martha Trump did not attend the funeral. Two deaths within a year profoundly affected the mood and behavior of the employees at the Institute. They became more appreciative of the opportunities offered at this rapidly developing site of research and patient care.

The events that took place seemed surreal as the shroud of mourning fell over the small close-knit community, and would never be forgotten. Not surprisingly, the death of either a family member or someone well-known in a community always brings sadness to those who personally knew and interacted with the deceased. The death of Dr. Meyer and Dr. Dellinger inevitably brought up feelings of sadness in the employees of the Department of Diagnostic Laboratories. Guilt intensified the grief of some who had had a contentious relationship with the doctors, and, in particular, because of the harsh comments they had made to the police and FBI.

Authorities informed Boris that he was no longer a target because of his involvement and disclosure of his research on viruses. This brought relief and an opportunity for him to renew his relationship with Clare.

The conversation between Clare and Boris at the very first opportunity reflected the whole situation in the Institute. Moreover, Boris said, "You know, Clare, Dr. Dellinger was killed because of me. They targeted me, but killed him, and because of this I feel terribly guilty. It seems that's the price for my freedom and the opportunity to do my favorite research. I'm very proud of becoming an American, and the only hope I have is that the results of my research will be successful and will benefit the country."

Clare said, "I understand your feelings, but you shouldn't torture yourself. You should see that Dr. Dellinger became a victim of the big war between the good and the evil. It is inevitable that the lives of Americans are often on the line in this struggle, and not only those of the military men and women in Iraq and Afghanistan, but also the lives of civilians, such as in New York in 2001 or in Boston in 2013, where even children became victims. Those were worldwide life-altering events. At least this time the whole story in which you were involved resulted in an important victory. The party guilty of violation of the previous international agreements has been exposed, along with the detection of the entire ring of foreign agents hidden in our country."

"I understand this situation intellectually, but I still don't feel comfortable, and I mourn the death of Dr. Dellinger."

Ironically, the next concert Clare and Boris attended featured the *Symphony Number Six* by Gustav Mahler. It was not planned originally, nor was it a coincidence that the symphony Mahler nicknamed 'Tragic' or the 'Tragic Symphony' was brought to Montana.

An anonymous influential and wealthy sponsor contacted Andrew Litton of Norway's Bergen Orchestra, who is famous for his performances of Mahler around the world, and suggested that he perform in Montana. The sponsor told Mr. Litton about the tragic events that had happened. It was not easy to make all the arrangements, including bringing in additional musicians, and situating the large orchestra that is required for this symphony on the rather small stage of the concert hall in Greeneville.

The reception of this complicated piece of music exceeded expectations. The first movement intended in major, but full of major-to-minor shifts, elicited feelings of darkness and melancholy. The second movement, as stated in Litton's explanation, feels like a heartache. Many perceived the themes of military marches throughout some parts of the symphony as a symbol of the inevitability of both good and evil events. Written at the beginning of the twentieth century, the symphony could have been perceived even as a prediction of tragic events during the twentieth century — two World Wars, Stalinism/Communism in Russia, Hitlerism in Germany, the Holocaust, etc. The most dramatic is the last movement, with drastic changes in mood and tempo, from optimistic to pessimistic themes, and most powerful blows. It ends in a dominating minor mood, also usually interpreted by experts as Mahler's intention to make this symphony a representation of life, in general.

There were three performances in Greeneville with barely enough room to accommodate all the people who wanted to attend. During the nearly one and a half-hour long performance, one could hear sounds of suppressed sobs through the deadly silence of the auditorium. The strong variable emotions triggered in the listeners by the music matched their mood, and completely exhausted many people. This performance helped many of them resolve their suffering, and it served as a requiem to the memories of Dr. Meyer and Dr. Dellinger. In the end, it was a wise idea to bring Mahler's symphony to this community.

The recent events and the concert brought Clare and Boris closer together. Boris resumed his research, and his publication in *Nature* brought him significant attention, nationally and internationally, along with attention to the Institute. The Institute received many requests from scientists who desired to visit the Institute. Clare continued her classes at the university, but busy schedules prevented them from taking needed vacations. Instead, they decided to take short breaks to travel through famous areas in Montana. That reinforced their feeling of 'belonging' and that was particularly important to Boris. After all the tragic events, it was important to feel that they were part of the state often referred to as 'The Land of the Shining Mountains.'

Despite being very busy with his work, Boris could not get away from his feeling of guilt. Memories of Dr. Dellinger and his death troubled him day and night. These thoughts even dominated over any appreciation that he, Boris, had miraculously escaped being killed. Observing his suffering, someone even suggested that Boris should obtain professional psychological counseling. Instead, Clare's attention and care appeared to be what Boris needed. She started calling him almost every day, and the phone conversations covered a broad range of topics, from daily news to books, music, and history. Most importantly was the way these topics were addressed by Clare. Her points were delivered in a softly vibrating voice with a genuine interest in Boris's opinion. It was obvious to Boris that Clare was falling in love with him, and Boris kept going through self-examination of his feelings. With his tough history and inherited stubbornness, it was not easy for him to admit that he was already in love with Clare. It was even more difficult to express his feelings, and to tell Clare that he was in love with her.

They continued taking short one-day trips, and did not stay anywhere overnight, but this would change soon. Clare became more and more interested in not only the history of Russia, but also in Russian culture, music, and literature, and Boris enjoyed discussing these subjects with her. In fact, he would enjoy any topic just to have the opportunity to talk and interact with Clare.

One story that especially impressed her was a story about Boris Pasternak. Clare saw the movie *Doctor Zhivago*, but did not know the dramatic story behind the novel, and was surprised by the events that surrounded its publication. Pasternak's poetry, which was widely published in English, deeply impressed Clare. Also, Boris presented Clare with a translation of Pasternak's famous poem called "A Candle of the Night," which was included in the *Doctor Zhivago* novel. He said, "The translation of this poem into English, written a few years ago, was dedicated to Dr. Ludmila Levina, who is dead now. Of course, the quality of this translation cannot be compared to Pasternak's masterful Russian writing, but it may impart the poignancy that Pasternak wished to convey in the original poem."

The days passed while Clare and Boris worked out the inevitable barriers that surfaced as their relationship advanced. Nevertheless, their lives became more and more intricately entwined as the days and weeks fell away. Finally, with some trepidation they went for a long weekend to the Powder River to ski and snowshoe. They stayed in a beautiful rustic cabin that was close to the riverbank. The one-room cabin had sparse amenities. There were two beds in opposite corners and a wood-burning fireplace in the middle of the wall. A large bearskin rug filled the space in the middle of the room, and the fireplace was giving the room a warm and cozy ambiance. The light from the lamp on the small table cast a golden glow in the room that made the freezing temperature outside only a memory. In the dresser drawer, Boris found a supply of candles and matches; a brass candleholder was the only other item in the dresser. Boris felt a level of comfort knowing the candles were there if he needed them, but he never expected to use them.

The first evening in the cabin snow began to fall, lightly, but suddenly turned heavy. The big flakes piled up rapidly. Clare and Boris, warmed by the crackling fire, watched the snow fall from inside the glowing cabin. They were warm and relaxed when suddenly the electricity went off. Boris went to the dresser, found the candles, and placed one in the holder. The whole situation became very similar to that in the Pasternak's poem, which Boris recited for Clare just a while before:

"The wind was blowing in all directions
And snow was covering the earth,
But in the house a candle of the night was burning on the table,
A candle of the night...
The flakes of snow have stormed the windows
To bring the memories of summer nights,
When swarms of midges and mosquitoes
Would fly to their fatal destination, attracted by the light,
The snow and frost attacked the windows
Designing on the glass some lines, and spots, and arrows,
But in the house a candle of the night was burning on the table,
A candle of the night...
A sound from falling tiny shoes
Has interrupted the silence of the night,
And melted wax, like tears, fell on the dress,
The tears from a candle of the night...
And shadows have appeared on the ceiling:
The shadows of crossed arms and legs,
The shadows of crossed destinations,
The shadows from a candle of the night...
The blizzard swallowed everything around
And things have vanished in the snowy darkness,
But in the house a candle of the night was burning on the table,
A candle of the night...
A draft from corners tried to strike the candle,
But like the shadows of the rising Angel's wings
The fire of temptation was rising in the air,
And still a candle on the table was burning through the night...
That February was a month of stormy blizzards,
And in the snowy nights, from time-to-time,
A candle in the house was burning on the table,
A candle of the night..."